The Call Girl Superheroine
A Torture Magic Universe Novel

By Douglas Todt

First Edition (2022)

The Call Girl Superheroine
A Torture Magic Universe Novel

By Douglas Todt

The Call Girl Superheroine
A Torture Magic Universe Novel
By Douglas Todt

Chapter One
The Working Girl
Saturday, March 27, 2021

As a call girl, I can tell you that getting screwed up the butt is like taking a big giant crap first thing in the morning — it doesn't always feel great, but it's gotta be done, and after it's over you feel a whole lot better, although for different reasons. As a, well, a superheroine, I can tell you that there's a *lot* worse things that can happen to you on a night in Vegas. At least as the call girl, I get paid. Not so much as the superheroine.

So, anyhow, here we are. I guess I gotta talk to you. I mean, fuck, you paid for this diary, right? Of course, you gotta realize sometimes you're talking to the Cube, the superheroine of Las Vegas, sometimes the hooker Shelby Starlight, and sometimes the real me, Shelby Burnbeck from Fullerton.

Anyhow, I'm sure what you want to know is obviously what the fuck the life of a call girl superheroine is like. Well . . . in a word — busy.

Anyhow, I started right out of high school as a call girl, although we aren't really call girls anymore. I mean, we book eighty percent online. Anyhow, that's fucking seminal. Or semantics. Not sure. Olivia would know. Regardless, whether you call me a call girl, hooker, prostitute, or whore, doesn't matter. Same job. So why do it? The money, of course. And the fact that . . . well, my background kind of led me to it. I needed a job to take care of myself, and that wasn't gonna happen at Burger King.

And I was pretty enough. I'm twenty-three now, by the way. I was born April 14, 1998. Back then, I had some chunky cheeks, a little body fat. I've toned that out. Now I'm a sleek five-eight chick with long, straight blonde hair parted in the middle with a few waves in it, don't mess with that look too much. I have blue eyes and a nice body. Imagine if you mix a 'girl next door' type with a good workout program and a stretching rack. Then you're close. But the real trick is my skin. A while back, I found out how to perfectly tan on the roof of my condo in just a thong. So, I have this long-legged, tight-assed body framed by a thong tan, and it drives men fucking nuts.

Anyhow, right at the moment, I'm at yet another hotel in Vegas. Which one doesn't matter, because once you're in the sack, they're all the fucking same.

So, this dude in yet another boring looking hotel room is slamming my backside hard. He's built. He's with the Falcons or Eagles or one of those bird teams. I'm not good with football. Anyhow, it's too bad he's not a Raider. The Raiders are the hottest thing to hit this town since the Rat Pack. If you're, like, eighty, you remember them.

"Uhhhhhhhhhhhh!" I moan, clutching the sheets as he drives into my ass really fuckin' deep. A lot of times during these jobs, I sort of zone out and plan my day or whatever. I've seen so many ugly white men in this job it would make a normal woman blind. Anyhow, this one is a little different. This due is built like a truck with muscles everywhere, a brick-shaped head, short black hair, perfect teeth, and he smells good. He can't have more than four percent body fat. And his member going up my backside is perfectly sized in length and girth.

I'm actually enjoying this one, which is, trust me, a rarity. If you really want to make a hooker happy, buy her a good dinner.

No, not really. I can't gain *any* weight. I mean, there's nothing worse than a fat hooker except for a fat superheroine trying to wedge her oversize ass into Kevlar. And besides, dinners for hookers usually get maudlin. We're like expensive bartenders. Guys dump on us about anything because they can wham-bam-thank-you-ma'am and get outta the room. Instead of drinking being their release, fucking relaxes them. In a way, it's sad how many of them have no one to talk to.

Yeah, so, usually, I don't get much into my job. It's a job, after all. I tell you, baby, you want to turn on a hooker, well, what gets us wet is having sex anyplace that is *not* a hotel room. I must spend eighty percent of my working hours in hotels or hotel restaurants. I had this rich old software tycoon for a time who rented a house out by Henderson. We fucked by the pool every day for two weeks. He was 62 and could only get it up with pills, but that was some of my best sex ever, laying there with my legs spread in the sun. Evan Baker, that was his name. I miss the old guy sometimes. I think he went back to New Jersey or one of those armpit places on the East Coast.

Sex is weird like that. Sex is the most bizarre invention of God, other than the platypus. I mean, it's fucking freaked out. It's best not to think about it too much.

"Is that nice, baby?" he asks.

"Yeah, yeah. Harder," I moan, thrusting back into him, watching us in the mirror. I admit, we look pretty hot.

So . . . being a call girl. Things to consider.

Advantage: the money is good. I mean, there are not many places a woman with no education can make six figures in a year . . . at least, not without being a tennis pro or a fashion model. I don't have to worry about car payments or utility bills or stupid stuff like that, and I'm not stuck flipping burgers at McDonald's to try and make ends meet. Major plus.

Disadvantage: the money isn't as good as you think. That three grand you gave me? The house gets half. So, I made $1,500, but out of that comes clothes, make-up, condiments, toys . . . the shit adds up, believe me. I'm a call girl, not some streetwalking whore. I spend time with the best, so I absolutely gotta look and be the best. I have more fucking clothes than a stage troupe.

Advantage: Every day is different. There's nothing boring about it. I get to meet people every day and every day I learn something. See, I'm not stupid. With my home life all fucked up and all, I never got to study like I should have, but I have brains. Just not in subjects that make you money. I was terrible in math and hard science. But anything to do with people, I aced those classes without even studying in high school — sociology, psychology, literature, even economics. Anything to do with how people think, I got that.

And that makes this job great because I meet so many people.

Disadvantage: You're always on the clock. Not having a set schedule means you must adapt to any schedule. That isn't always fun.

Advantage: I stay in shape, although it's a major effort to keep this body looking this good. I work out at least four days a week, and usually have sessions of kickboxing on Monday, Wednesday, and Friday. At least that's free. My kickboxing instructor and I worked out an agreement, if you know what I mean. Anyhow, it's exhausting.

And food . . . oh, God, there are days I would kill for, like, a hot dog. Or a chocolate doughnut. But I can't cheat. Ever. Blow one or two days and suddenly your ass is bigger than a two-car garage.

Disadvantage: Okay, people are gross. Generally, men are much more gross than women, because we at least care, but that's not always true. Obviously, in my job as a call girl, I'm mostly being intimate with men. Well, the male gender, 'cause some of these guys aren't classy enough to call men. A few rules, guys. One, wear deodorant. You smell. Two, take a shower before banging us.

This one is major. No one likes an icky-dickie, but dirty people are gross in general. One girl at the Empire, she requires a shower as part of or before any session. That's a little extreme. But, seriously guys, make an effort.

Oh, three, cut your toenails and fingernails. You're not baboons. There's lots of others, but those are the main ones.

Advantage: it can be fun. You can figure that one out. But aside from the obvious, it's nice sometimes to do something weird sexually without having to worry about how the other person it gonna take it.

Disadvantage: it can be dangerous. Now, it's not nearly that much so for me. I mean, if someone gets too rough, a little wind or earth channeling shakes his dick up and gets him settled. But most of us in this business have been at least slapped around once or twice, if not threatened with knives, guns, and — in one case, not mine — a welding torch. That one is a long story.

Advantage: Let's get back to money. Okay, you want another one? I've been at this long enough to set my own terms, own schedule, and who I want to work with.

Disadvantage: Diseases. Yeah, even with condoms, I've had some stuff come down. Had the clap twice in the last few months. I don't think about AIDS or anything like that. Does a wide receiver think about a linebacker ready to take his head off? He sure the fuck doesn't if he wants to keep his job.

So, there's life as a call girl.

Now, let me explain how Las Vegas works. We want your money.

Technically, prostitution is illegal here, but that's mostly so that some streetwalking, cum-bucket whore doesn't set up camp on a corner and offend some old tourist from Iowa, or so the cops can arrest some dim-bulb broad usin' her assets for trafficking, be it drugs or human. Underneath that, the mob wants us all working for the agencies. That's where they make their money. It's how the control us.

Anyhow, most hookers are addicted to something; drugs, booze, even sex, or if not addicted, stuck with kids with no daddy around. But even those of us that aren't, and that's maybe one in five, we all have one common addiction, but it's an acceptable one — money. Cold, hard cash. We all want the money, and the money is what drives our decisions. As I said, a lot of girls have kids and shit. The rest of us are just greedy. I mean, I *am* greedy. I don't want to count on a man to take care of me like my mother did. If I'm going to take it up the backside, I'm going to be properly rewarded.

Vegas has two rules.

One, money rules. Money determines everything here. In the last twenty years or so, all this tourist marketing bullshit has made the image of Vegas as this town where you can do anything and is still family friendly. Most of it is marketing shit, but at the end of the day, you really can do anything here. Yes, you can. It just *costs* you.

Two, Vegas is a night town. This is just a matter of practicality. For like six months of the year the daytime temperature is triple digits. You go out when it's 108 degrees and see if you want to hang around. And fuck that shit about it being a dry heat.

Now days, Vegas on the strip is all interlocked so timid tourists from Minnesota with no tan can survive walking around all day in 107-degree heat. That's the obvious thing.

What's not so obvious to people not on the inside here is how everything is like a fucking maze. There are all kinds of secret entrances, exits, and passages. Remember, this town was built by the mob. And there are some more benign reasons for the secrecy. It's nice to get dead people out of their hotel room without being observed by everyone. It's nice to let ladies like me into certain areas without being seen. It's also better security.

Anyhow, once you know all of these passages and tricks, no one ever sees you — unless you want them to, of course. Some guys like that showy aspect. They get a piece of ass and flaunt her, unaware every local in town knows he's just a horny old man that can't get a woman on his own. But you know about boys and their tiny egos. I usually go in the front door, no problem.

That's Vegas in a nutshell. Housing is cheap. You can build fucking condos into the desert forever here. Still, it's going up fast. Everyone is fucking retiring here now. Anyhow, I don't care about that, 'cause I have a nice place. I was able to buy a condo by my second year . . . in cash. It's not much, but it's a starter, you know?

It's off Hacienda drive, just off the strip. One bedroom, 950 square feet, second floor, cost 99K. It's a pink building with desert landscape, pretty tacky exterior, but nice inside. I spent most of time inside in bed, frankly, with my two cats. Yeah, cats. I have a wild, female orange cat named Popsicle and her older brother, Shy. He has a big head. She's fast as a whip. Cats are good pets. They keep to themselves and don't demand much. Besides, if I didn't have them, I'd probably have something dumb like a bird or a turtle.

It is a bit small, only because of my clothes. I am at the point where I have clothes hanging in portable hangers in the living room. What can I do?

The main thing is . . . it's *mine*. I've had multiple offers to buy me condos and become the other woman. Multiple offers to have homes and stuff in other countries. But I'm not a fool. Those offers come with a price. I know how to take care of myself. I've had to ever since . . . since childhood shit, okay? Back off.

Anyhow, Vegas is a place with powerful men with lots of money, but also idiots without a lot of money trying to act like they do. Either can be a pain in the ass, literally. Dealing with the guys means dealing with powerful people with a lot of money who like to be in charge. Sometimes being in charge means exerting, shall we say, physical force.

Granted, the Empire, my agency, is a very class act. Nina, the owner, she doesn't put up with much. But that doesn't help you if some asshole breaks the rules and breaks your arm or stabs out your eye with a potato peeler before you can get help.

We have a lot of security. I have security within fifty yards. But that's a long way in an emergency. Way too far.

So . . . a girl's gotta take care of herself sometimes. Channeling isn't always the most effective defense. I know self-defense, but the main defense is to defuse any hostility. Be in charge, but don't let 'em know it. After all, they are stupid men.

The really dangerous ones are the sly ones. They're the ones that want total control. They'll dose you with paralysis drugs and all sorts of crap that leave you like a rag doll, then start sticking their thing in places that you sure the fuck don't want it.

There are some basic rules to follow. Don't eat or drink anything they offer or bring with them. Don't use their toys, protective devices, or lubricants. But still . . . there are limits to how much you can protect yourself.

I'll tell you more about that in a bit . . . because I'm about to cum.

I yelp and clutch the sheets as I have a powerful anal orgasm. It stops him from plowing me, I get so tight.

"Damn, girl!" he says.

I moan and see stars. After an eternity, he continues, and he shoots really quick, turned on by the fact that I'm turned on. His name is Delvin, nice guy, hope his team has a good season.

When we're done, he pops out and I lay on my side. "That was fun. You have a skill at this."

He laughed. "So do you. How much time is left?"

I cocked my head. "Twelve minutes, Delvin. But I'll clock out if you want to take me to a late lunch for just the price of a meal. I'm fucking starving."

"Deal. You let guys have pictures?"

"Nope," I said immediately. Some girls did. They charged for them. I didn't really care if some guy whacked his willie to my photo, though it tends to cut down repeat business. My concern was some dude having my photo and doing things to it to make me look like, I don't know, like I eat poop or something. Besides, being the Cube, the less pictures out there of me the better. Can you imagine my superheroine career ending because my identity was exposed by some john? I'd never live it down.

"Aw, well, that's okay. C'mon, let's roll."

I really had to get something to eat. Saturday was always a huge day for the service, but I was technically offline this week. My trip as the Cube to New Mexico had wrapped up early, so I took this call as a favor to Nina. So, I could do what I wanted, and I wanted a lunch. And Delvin was fun to talk to, unlike a lot of guys in my line of work.

I had a meeting with Olivia before a meet as the Cube with Charlie Sanders later tonight. Had I any idea of what the evening was gonna be like, I would have stayed with Delvin and let him do me up the ass again. It would've been easier.

Chapter Two
Stalking the Stalker

Today is March 27, 2021. It's a year to the day since that asshole Davis kidnapped me. So, I was in a pissy mood. The football guy helped with the mood, but that wore off fast.

However, I didn't have time to feel sorry for myself. My BFF, Olivia, needed help. Time to switch roles, compartmentalize they call it, and think like the Cube.

I met her at the Magic House. It's this world-famous magic place that's north of the strip, still Las Vegas Boulevard but closer to North Las Vegas where the town is more like, well, a town than a circus. And a bit run down, honestly. If you've ever watched "Pawn Stars" and been to their shop, the Magic House is a bit north of that but before the 515. Anyhow, magicians operate there, famous ones I guess, but it also serves as a school and a place for apprenticeships, and that's why I was there today.

The Magic House had a weird, pointed roof, big red letters, and looked like a castle from the outside. Inside, it was a typical theatre and held about a thousand people.

Anyhow, the place didn't run live shows. The theatre was for training classes. This being a late Saturday afternoon, the place was dead. But there was a yellow '18 Kia Stinger in the parking lot, so I knew my BFF since high school and the first girl I ever kissed, Olivia Young, was inside.

The main door was locked, so I buzzed the intercom. Then I heard her voice. Olivia always talked in precise, clipped words, sort of like a machine. And she had this British accent that was totally fucking fake but was smooth like coffee and sounded really sexy. "Shelby?"

"Yeah."

"Good work, girl, you are right on time. Hold on."

I looked at my watch. "It's 3:02. Technically, I'm two minutes late."

"Shut it."

The door opened into a lobby and standing on a red carpet near a bunch of potted palm plants was Olivia. She was in one of her many magician's outfits. This one had thigh-high black boots, black nylons underneath that. Her torso was covered by a formal, black jacket; a white button-down bodice, and a black swimsuit that served as panties. Her earrings were red balls, her lipstick red, her mascara perfect.

Olivia was pretty, sporting light brown hair that was fairly short and swept to the left of her face, a cute little cut. Her eyes were her best feature, these ancient sky-blue eyes. She had a good figure and kept in shape. She had no choice. Being a magician was a lot of fucking work. Her skin was lightly tanned. She was just a tad shorter than me, and very slim. The main difference was she'd had breast implants and I was all natural. Not as big, but natural.

I entered the lobby, and we hugged. I could smell her perfume, but also her perspiration. She had obviously been rehearsing. One thing I learned early on from her, stage work is hard. The lights are hot, and the activity is like frickin' martial arts.

"You look good," she said. "How was New Mexico?"

I frowned.

Studying me, she asked, "Do you want to talk about it?"

Shaking my head, I looked away. Olivia was closer to me than a sister. We talked and texted every day even when we were apart. She knew I was the Cube, knew I was a channeler, and knew a lot about the paranormal 'cause she was a necromancer . . . I'll explain that shit later. Anyhow, I had spent the last two days as the Cube in Bumfuck,

New Mexico tracking down a serial killer who liked to kidnap and eat children. I stopped him . . . it wasn't pretty.

"Later?" she prodded.

"Later. What's been happening here? Your text said you had a problem. The owner pinching your ass?"

Now she looked reluctant. Leading me to the stage, she sat on the edge, getting dust on her boots. I had changed after fucking Delvin or Devin, whatever his fucking name was, and was wearing faded blue jeans, a white sweatshirt, and a brown purse, purely casual. We made an incongruous pair.

I leaned against the side of the stage and cocked my head. "Why so shy?"

She made a face like a kid drinking bad medicine. "I'm . . . I'm being *stalked*."

"Isn't that normal?" I said with a smile. Entertainers were stalked every day.

"It's different. It's weird."

Now I was worried. "Weird? Paranormal?"

She sighed with exasperation at herself, not me. "Maybe. I'm not a fool, Shelby, or paranoid. The last couple of weeks I've been finding . . . things moved. And it seems like at least once a day, I'm finding . . . something unsettling in a private space; my dressing room, my apartment complex, even my fucking car."

"Did they scratch the paint?" I asked, trying to relax her with a joke. She loved her fucking car, which I bought for her, by the way, and with cold, hard cash.

"God, no! No . . . okay. Okay, I'm gonna put it out there, and then you can tell me my mother fucked up my head and I'm crazy."

She paused, so I said, "Okay."

"I'm being stalked . . . by the marionette."

What the fuck do you say to that?

Olivia is my best friend and mentor, really. This is the person I call if I'm having a bad cramps day or have the hospital call if I'm in a coma. She is my BFF in the extreme.

And she is smart as a whip.

And now she's telling me *this*. Now, even in the paranormal, I've never heard of a marionette actually being alive.

"You seem . . . shocked," said Olivia finally.

"I just . . . a puppet?"

"Marionette. Marionettes are on strings. Puppets are things you put your hands into."

I frowned. "Explain how you think he's stalking you? What is he? Is he yours?"

Using her phone, she showed me a picture. "This is Woody."

I frowned. Woody was a marionette who had strings but no controls. He wore a tuxedo with a red bow tie and looked perpetually happy. Short red hair, freckles, and wide blue eyes made him creepy, yes. Anything that is perpetually happy is creepy anyhow.

As I examined the photo, she said, "He's a new part of my act. I pretend to animate him with the controls, then I let them go and he starts walking. That's because he's battery controlled and can walk and talk."

"I've never seen that act."

"I just came up with it last month, haven't put it out yet, been trying it out. Anyhow, I've found him in . . . really odd places the last couple of days in particular. He's turned up in my room, the bathroom, my magician's box, and even the backseat of my car."

She looked scared. I nodded and said, "Someone is fucking with your head. Who has access to him?"

"No one. I keep him locked up in the effects box, which is this big-ass chestnut cabinet in the dressing room."

"Nothing else disturbed or missing?"

Shaking her head, she said, "And I took the batteries out."

"Puppets don't walk."

"Marionette. And you know we've both seen stranger shit."

She had me there. Frowning, I said, "Where is he now?"

Nodding at the door, she said, "In my dressing room."

Olivia's dressing room was, well, messy. Olivia was generally neat, but she shared the room with two other acts, and they were often changing at a moment's notice. Picture a small theater dressing room covered in bras and weird stretchy pants, and you have it.

The chestnut cabinet was in the corner under a pile of yoga pants and a white jacket. I removed them and found a combination lock. Olivia reached past me and opened it.

"Don't trust me with the combination?" I asked playfully. I knew she trusted me with everything.

She pointed at her ear. "The walls have ears sometimes."

I nodded, figuring she was worried we were bugged — not an illegitimate fear given she was being stalked. I was sure something was up, but I was also confident the puppet or whatever wasn't moving on its own.

Yeah, I've been wrong before. But not this time . . . at least, so I thought for about twenty seconds.

Once the cabinet opened, I lifted the lid and peered into the dark interior. I found Woody and lifted him out.

I studied him and here is where being a call girl would have left me clueless and being a superheroine had its uses. One thing channelers and all paranormals can do is sense and analyze auras. That's the soul, your life-force if you're a moronic atheist. Anyhow, as I touched Woody, I felt a tingle.

Focusing my vision, I sensed a *human* aura. Auras are seen as colors, and a balanced individual will be like a rainbow. Woody was a rainbow, but with a slightly dominant brown-tanish color. This color indicated someone that was a methodical overthinker, someone seen as uptight and elusive. Evasive? One of those stupid words.

I stepped back, careful not to betray the fact that I had sensed an aura. Woody was clearly some type of mystical being like myself, so I had to hope he hadn't sensed that I could sense his true nature. I didn't want a fight with him here and now for two reasons. One, I didn't know his abilities. Two, his colors were wrong for a dangerous stalker. That would be someone angry or exerting sexual vigor — we're talking red and orange here.

Was he a spy?

I dumped him back inside and locked the box. I looked at Olivia. She knew about auras, of course, being a necromancer. She just wasn't as adept at sensing this stuff. But I also got just a flash, and then it was hidden. Since I'm after guys like Davis all the time, I'm used to TMs and others hiding their auras. TMs are torture magicians, use the pain and adrenaline from torture to convert aural energy into telekinetic force. I'll explain more about these sick fucks later. Anyhow, mostly, I also didn't want her to inadvertently tip off Woody. Sending Woody to stalk Olivia didn't make much sense, especially with his aura. Something weirder was going on.

I nodded and said, "I gotta pee. You got a pisser in this place?"

Olivia knew that I knew where the bathroom was, but she played up to me and pointed at the door. I moved, she didn't, so I said, "Come with me. We'll talk on the way."

She gave me a look, and although she clearly wasn't certain what was going on, she followed me. Once we were in the hallway, she said sarcastically, "What, you forget how to pee by yourself? Or do you need me to wipe your ass?"

"Oh, shut up and follow me."

I moved to the men's restroom just outside the theatre. I saw her stop and start to protest, so I simply grabbed her wrist and pulled and said, "I'll explain inside."

Once we were inside, Olivia made a face. "Place is gross."

Looking around, I said, "It's clean."

"It's been used by men. It's gross. Why are we here?"

"I figure you've been bugged. The one place they certainly aren't going to put a bug to listen to you is in the men's restroom."

Her face showed surprise, then a sly smile. "You're smart. I knew there was a reason I kept you around."

I winked and said, "I thought you just kept me around to give you head."

"Oh, bite me," she said with a smirk.

I laughed. "Let's talk serious. I sense something in that wooden fucker. So you *aren't* crazy."

"*Something*?" she asked, her eyes growing wide.

"An aura. I don't know how, but there's some type of life inside him."

Her eyes widened, and she slammed a fist into her hand. "I knew it! I knew he was a peeping tom piece of shit!" Then she looked worried. "But how? Is he really a midget?"

"No, it's more the shit I get into than necromancy or zombie stuff. Paranormal aura all the way."

"Yeah, well, I can see that. Well, BFF, you're the superheroine now. You're the Cube. What do we do?"

"Let's go back to your dressing room. Follow my lead."

"Got it."

We returned. As we entered, I said, "So that's what I think. I think someone just wants to scare you. So, we set a trap."

"How do we do that?"

"I'm not sure, and I have a date tonight. Let's go home, sleep on it, and regroup tomorrow."

"What do we do with the marionette?"

I shrugged and stared at Woody, who innocuously stared back. I couldn't help but think that a thousand horror films started with little wooden fucks like him, but I pushed that thought aside. That was speculation and didn't fit the facts. "Leave his ass here. He's just a fucking puppet."

"Marionette."

I kicked him and said, "Whatever. He's not real. C'mon, let's go home."

We left.

Once we were outside, she stared at the door for a long time and finally remotely unlocked her car as she said, "I dunno about this."

"Let's go talk about it. Your place or mine?"

"Mine's closer."

"Fine. I'll meet you there. I gotta stop and get gas on the way."

She kissed my cheek. "Thanks, Shelby."

"NP BFF."

Once I was in the car, I turned up the music. I listen to a lot of different music, 'cause I'm a different type of girl. When I'm hooking, I like rap, hard rock, up tempo shit. When I'm with Olivia, or someone close, I like classical. When I'm driving in the car, I usually settle on generic rock, you know, whatever's trendy. That's what I went with tonight. Lady Gaga.

I stopped and got gas and an energy drink, then met Olivia at *her* condo. It was the end unit on a two-story, eight unit building on one of those new roads they've been building west of town, pushing out into the endless desert. The place was white stucco red trim, desert landscape. It was new, but small and cheap.

I had the code to the security gate, of course. I went up the back stairs and to the right to reach the door to her unit. I knocked, no answer, so I used my key.

"Olivia?"

No answer, but I heard her moving around in the bedroom. I went to meet her, one of the more dangerous tasks of my life, 'cause Olivia is not exactly the neatest person around. She's always busy and always has magic shit everywhere, but she's also, okay, well, just a fucking slob sometimes. And clearly, being hassled by Woody the last few days made it worse, because the place was as messy as I've ever seen it.

I entered a living room covered in dirty clothes, unwashed dishes, and plants hanging from the ceiling. There were catalogues about costumes everywhere. For some reason, Olivia was into catalogues. They helped her find deals, because she went through a lot of clothes. She had a yellow sofa covered with a purple blanket, a lot of pictures of her on stage, a painting of a tiger in the wild, and all sorts of small, flat tables. She had magic props on a lot of them.

The kitchen was small. There were a few brown cabinets, a fridge, a microwave over the oven, and not much else. The décor was black, white, and stainless steel for the appliances, with backsplash that was black with white stars. Backsplash is important. Hers sucked.

I moved to the bedroom. Yikes. When I got to the bedroom, she was down to her bra and panties and looking for some leggings. She was fucking wound up and clearly anxious. I went to her and put a hand on her shoulder and said, "Hey, relax. I got this. This is shit I can handle, unlikely pretty much anything else."

Trusting me, she smiled and kissed me quickly. "I know. That's why I called you. I just don't . . . I don't like any of this."

"No one likes being stalked, except maybe crazy Hollywood actresses who are no longer relevant and want their name in the paper," I said. As she slipped on a pair of dark green leggings, I gave her a mock look of suspicion and said, "Hmmmmm . . . or crazy Vegas magicians!"

Rolling her eyes, she said, "If I wanted publicity, I'd run naked along the 15 at rush hour."

I laughed. "I'd pay to see *that*."

"Naw, then I'd being doing *your* job. Well, the job of Shelby Starlight. Speaking of which, you *did* you work today?" she asked, putting on a black blouse that had pictures of stars.

"Yep, Nina asked as a favor. Got backdoored by a football player and cleared three grand and got a nice lunch. I've had worse days."

She rocked her head back and forth. "Not too shabby. I take it being sodomized was better than being in Deming?"

I made a face like I was going to vomit. "*Anything* is better than New Mexico. Eating out of a dumpster is better than that place."

"It can't be *that* bad," she said, leading me to the kitchen. I knew she didn't want sex or comfort, she was too wound up. She just needed to talk and eat.

Not that we had sex a lot these days. I guess you'd say we were friends with benefits, but our relationship was a lot more complex than that. We had sex maybe once every few weeks these days, just when we were in the mood or really needed comfort. There's a lot of reasons . . . I mean, we both want to find Mr. Right someday. Gotta keep that avenue open. My job also gets in the way. I mean, it's hard to come home and want sex after being slammed like a hamburger patty. But mostly, it's Olivia's travels. She's got her magic act really going. She covers all the Pacific and Southwest of the country, and even goes out of country sometimes to, like, Vancouver and Tijuana and even Baja. Anyhow, I was glad she wasn't in the mood. I wasn't either. I was a little wound up about Woody myself.

"So, this Delvin's a football player? Who's he with?" she asked, handing me a Coors light. She had a Bud.

"Fuck if I know. It was a bird team."

"I'll find him," she said. I wasn't up on sports. I could sort of converse a bit, because I talked to guys all day, but they didn't interest me. Olivia was more into it.

"He plays for the Cardinals. He's pretty good. He's a running back and had 1,200 yards rushing last year."

"That means nothing to me."

She smiled. "He ranked sixth in the league. The league has 32 teams."

"That is pretty good," I said, now interested. "He seemed to like me."

"Keep your butt ready," she said with a wink.

As we sat looking up Delvin's stats, the phone rang. Nina. She's my boss at the agency . . . that stuff's private. Anyhow, she only calls if it's important, so I immediately answered. "Yo, boss?"

"Shelby, I know I already called you in as a favor today."

"Need another?" I asked with a very positive attitude. I like money, but I could also sense the exasperation in Nina's voice. She was this fifty-ish woman with a round face and short, blonde hair who had a real masculine voice, but right now she was squeaking, indicating stress.

"Sure do. Can you take a quickie and peg some guy?"

This wasn't the first time my careers as call girl and superheroine had collided. The Cube had a meeting at eleven with the guy I mentioned, Charlie Sanders, to hopefully get info on Davis' whereabouts. I knew Davis was back in town but hadn't managed to track him down. Right now, it was 8:30.

Now, I was a high-ranking whore at the agency. I could say no to Nina, and no one would hold it against me, especially since I already did a favor today. But pegging was easy money and would get me further on Nina's good side, which I might need.

Olivia was always the Cube's backup on these meets. Sadly, she didn't have a cool code name. I could pull this off, but I would have to have her to help me with timing.

This ran through my head really quick. There was barely a pause before I put up a caution hand to Olivia, who started to pay attention, and I said, "Yup. Where and when?"

"ASAP at the Luxor. He wants a blonde and Cindy is his favorite, but she isn't done her seven o'clock yet and Candy and Melissa won't pick up the fucking phone," said Nina, clearly annoyed.

"I'm on it. Text me details."

"Thanks. I owe you. This one is all yours. Have fun!"

I hung up. What she meant was no house payment, so that told me this was a *very* important client. I turned to Olivia. "I gotta go on a call, but it will be fast. The Cube has gotta make that meet with Charlie."

Olivia nodded. "I'm ready. What do you need?"

"Just be there and be ready. Be ready for last second changes."

She laughed. "I'm a magician. I'm ready for anything!"

"Ready, little boy?" I asked as I knelt behind my client, trick, john, customer, whatever you wanna call him.

"Yup."

"Okay. Hold on."

I drove my black plastic strap-on cock into him gently, 'cause he seemed a little tight.

Like I said, pegging was easy money and it had become a big thing in recent years. I used a strap-on once with Olivia, but it wasn't our normal thing. They were tricky to use. If they were too tight, they made your guts feel like, squished. And too loose and you'd lose the momentum. The straps and buckles were all different, depending on how much they had been used.

I had my own, but this guy wanted me to use his, so I was getting used to it as I slowly moved back and forth.

The pegging thing . . . one of my first calls was with this girl named Sandy Sands. She was a pretty good hooker, but she liked the blow too much and eight months into her career she wound up doing five years for selling cocaine. Anyhow, she was one of my riders on an early call, back when I still had to pair up as a rookie. Rookie hookers are like rookie cops, they always work in pairs until the house knows the girl can handle herself.

Anyhow, I thought pegging was weird, but Sandy said most of them were guys in their 40s and 50s whose testosterone levels were dropping, so they were getting into more passive sex. Taking it up the butt for a guy does not make him gay. It just means he has a very happy prostate and found out. Apparently for guys, the prostrate is like our g-spot, which does exist, boys.

Me personally, if I was a guy, I'd just find another guy with a big unit and do it the right way, but a lotta guys have this thing about being gay.

Now, some are into it for dominance. It's their way of submitting.

And some, a few, have this sort of mommy fetish that must go back to childhood. Men are really very fragile creatures. The slightest thing can trigger their hormones and they have this fetish for life. It's kind of sad.

Harry here fits into the last category.

Now, when pegging a guy, it's a little tricky. That thing stuck in him is not me. I can't feel how tight he is, how much he's spasming on it. As you must know if you read the first page, I'm into anal. Anal is not something that is perfect every time. A lot of people aren't into it because of that. Olivia never got into it. She tried it once and said she felt constipated for a week. Anyhow, since I can't feel him, I have to go very slow at first to make sure he's taking it. The butt isn't designed to stretch from exterior penetration. You're reversing the flow, and that can make it hurt.

But you can tell from most of them once they get into it that it feels good.

Harry is shaped like a typical white, 51-year-old man — like a bald pineapple. He must go 250 and has a big, fat, white belly. Trust me, this physique is probably sixty percent of my customers. No, more like seventy. Some weeks, it seems like that's all I've seen, fat bellies. But it doesn't bug me, because for me this is a job.

Anyhow, I start slamming him pretty good. "You take it from mommy, little boy!" I shout, he having told me this is what likes.

I learned very early on, their fantasy is just that, their fantasy. Not *mine*, not yours. Doesn't matter how fucking weird it is — okay, there are some limits — but for the most part, it's just harmless fun.

Pegging is fun. It's easy. No sex, so no disease worries, and it's a decent workout which will earn me pizza after the Cube meets with Charlie.

Harry starts stroking himself and I tell him, "If you cum, you have to eat it off the floor. Those are mommy's rules."

"Uh, yes, yes, I'll do it."

All I can figure is the guy got caught jacking off as a kid and his mom made him eat it to deter him, which just created this weird fetish. I've seen weirder. Guys are, as I've said, very fragile. Almost anything can turn into a fetish for them.

Anyhow, once we finish up, I'm off to find Charlie. Which means moving my ass fast, because this took longer than planned.

I'm a typical woman. I'm *always* fucking running late.

Chapter Three
The Meet with Charlie

Racing, I got into the Kevlar in my car in the hotel parking lot and raced outta there like I was in one of those lame-ass *Fast and Furious* movies. Trust me, people got outta my way. Hey, Vegas people are used to crazy drivers. My car, by the by, is a '21 BMW Z4 painted bright blue. The sales guy has a standing freebee with me anytime he wants it.

Anyhow, the mall where I was meeting Charlie had four stores under a united white front with a Spanish-style awning and a small parking lot. There was a *Round Two* Sporting Goods store, which sold used sporting goods; a Dollar Store; a Domino's; and finally, a pawn shop. I got to the sporting goods store at 11:07, only a few minutes late. Olivia's Stinger was parked on the side of the now almost empty mall next to a silver Honda that I figured was Charlie's. I parked next to her. Olivia saw me and got out of the Stinger. The only other cars were a handful out front, all clustered around the Domino's and the pawn store, which was open 24 hours.

I parked and exited, dressed as the Cube. Olivia wore a jeans jacket, jeans, and facial mascara that made her look almost dead. She said, "You're late, but Charlie hasn't come out."

"Good. I figured he wouldn't." I rolled my eyes. "I know he needs the cash."

"You sure you're good with me out here?"

"Yep."

"You safe with him?"

"Yep. I told you, I used to fuck him. His brother owns a bar. But Charlie sucked as a bartender and his brother canned him. I did Charlie a few times at half-rate, but when he couldn't afford that, I hadd'a cut him off. So, I know him as Shelby. He's actually a decent guy."

Olivia gave me a look. "Keep your guard up."

"You bet."

I went to the rear, where an alley behind the mall led to two loading docks and rear entrances for all the stores. The alley had seen better days. I'm pretty sure some of the potholes went all the way through to China.

The back door was old and wooden but had a new lock. It was, however, unlocked as planned. I entered. Obviously, the store was closed, but the back stockroom was well lit and had several benches around a soda machine and candy machine, a sort of break room. Charlie was sitting at a cheap plastic table.

"Wow! It *is* you! Hi, Cube!" he said, rising with wide eyes.

Twenty-six-year-old Charlie Sanders was a very short man at five-five. He had curly black hair with a matching beard and wide, brown eyes. He was suntanned and not unattractive, though sort of skinny and lacking definition, like a used condom.

Clearing my throat, I stood in the doorway and said with a horribly fake masculinity, "Are we alone?"

He had risen and pushed the chair back, but hadn't moved, so he was about ten feet in front of me. "Yeah."

"Let's talk out back," I said, not thrilled with the close quarters.

"Sure"

We went out back. There were a few cars for employees — like I said, the Domino's and the pawn shop were still open. Vegas is a night town, baby. Deal with it. Anyhow, one was a black Mazda 626 that had to be twenty years old. Charlie sat on it. The paint was faded form the sun, and it had a long scrape down the passenger side from wheel to wheel.

In the Kevlar, I had a lot of pockets. One was above my left boob. I pulled from it $1,300 dollars. "We agreed on $1,000. I'm bringing extra because I've heard from others you're a reliable source."

His eyes lit up at the sight of cold, hard cash. I usually get that look when guys see my tits. Hey, I have a nice rack. But Charlie clearly needed the cash. He was almost drooling as he nodded and said, "Sure, sure. I'm good."

"What do you know?"

"Davis. Okay, my brother, Scott, he owns the Night Shift bar over off Tropicana. The old part, we serve locals mostly. I used to bartend, but he fired me, which is why I sell used soccer balls now." He rolled his eyes. "Anyhow, I was in visiting the other night. I follow all your social media stuff, and I saw this guy, he's on your site, this Davis guy. He was talking to Scott, bitching about some of his warehouse shipments being fucked up by customs and being in a bind. You know, bartenders hear everything."

"I know," I said.

"So . . . I mean, what Davis said was he had to move the goods fast and was looking for manpower at five-hundred bucks an hour.

Whoa. "*Five bills?*"

"Yeah. Fuck, half the bar emptied out. I went with him. I know this man was Davis. But I don't know anything else. He took a look at me and cut me out, too skinny."

"Where's the warehouse?"

He handed me the address. Then he said, "There's one other thing. I, uhmm, found this thing at Scott's bar." He reached into his front pocket and pulled out a small gemstone about the size of a fingernail. It glowed a brilliant green. It was almost hypnotizing.

"Scott said Davis gave him this in lieu of cash two weeks ago. Scott fell asleep at the bar and dreamed he was on Venus and almost suffocated, so he gave it to me. I fell asleep and thought I was drowning, so I want to be rid of it. I figure if you're a super-hero, you might know what it is or be able to use it."

I held it. Then I slipped it into my pocket, confident it wasn't a tracer or mini-bomb or some Lex Luthor type shit. It was a gem, a totem. I'll explain more later. "Thanks. Consider your extra $300 the payment. If this pans out, I'll bring you back another thousand."

He looked thrilled. "Damn. Thanks. I mean, I hope you get him. He seems like a real douche."

"You have no idea. Later."

He nodded. I left, and he went back inside. I rounded the building and found Olivia sitting in the car using her phone to post on the Cube's instant media sites. I had no fucking time for the Cube's instant media. I had my own account to manage. And Olivia seemed to enjoy it, and being an entertainer, she had a flair for it.

She looked up. "How'd it go?"

I smiled. "Oh, really well. I think I know where fuck-face is. And I have cold, hard cash left over from the peg-job. Want pizza?"

She exited the Stinger. "You fucking bet."

We walked around the front to the Domino's. Yes, I was still the Cube. But you have to remember, this is Vegas, and now that Cosplay is so popular, it's not all that weird in this town to walk around dressed up even when it's not damn fucking Halloween. Besides, Olivia was with me and looked pretty normal.

Just as we rounded the corner, I was about to take off my mask when a delivery driver, just a kid, exited his car, having presumably returned from a delivery. He had a beat-up Toyota Corolla that was brown with a gray passenger side door, and the kid was pimple city with glasses and God-awful black hair.

A bald dude with a red Cardinals hoodie and baggie jeans stepped out of the red pickup next to him and shoved him to the ground, then took his cash pouch. Just like that. In broad . . . well, not daylight, but right under the lights. But there was no one else outside.

"Hey!" yelped the kid as he fell into a planter with a cactus and got stuck in the butt. Hey, delivery is a risky business. It's as bad as hooking.

I moved instantly. I left my mask on and ran across the driveway towards the pickup, which had started.

Then I channeled earth and did it in a jerking, earthquake fashion. The pickup went up and down almost instantly, and the cracking pavement popped the tires. I was pretty proud of that one. That wasn't easy.

"Fuck me!" shouted the Cardinals' robber. As he exited, I raced over. He didn't even notice me, because he was moving to steal Pimple Boy's delivery car.

I got there first. "You're under arrest!"

I then kicked him in the balls, making those kickboxing lessons pay off big-time.

"Whooooooooooooooofffffffffffffff!" he gasped, put his hands on his groin, and collapsed.

Suddenly, the workers at Domino's and the pawn shop headed for me.

I said, "Security cameras should be enough to give our bird-loving friend here a night in jail."

Then I ran the other way. There were about six people taking pictures with their phones, but they were all so surprised that they didn't chase us, thank God.

Olivia saw me coming, turned, and got the Stinger started. Then we raced out of the alley.

I ripped off my mask. "Holyyyyyyyy fuck! Hah! Did you see him drop!"

She laughed. "I'm sure his face will be all over the internet once the Domino's clerks pull the parking lot footage. You think my car is safe?"

"Cameras don't extend around the end or the back, part of the reason I met Charlie back there," I said.

In the Stinger, we were blocks away within the snap of a finger. I gotta tell you, the Stinger is a cool car. It's sporty but practical, much like Olivia herself.

By the time we got home to my condo, which was closer, I'd wound down a little and changed into a white camisole and jeans. We never did get our pizza, so we ate leftover grilled chicken and watched an episode of *The Great* on Hulu. Olivia liked it. I was okay with it.

It finished around 1:45 in the morning. I stretched and said, "I have to shower before bed. Running around in Kevlar in Vegas is like wearing a winter coat on Miami Beach. Flexible my ass."

She laughed. "Okay. Mind if I crash here? I have nothing to do tomorrow. I have that trip to Tahoe starting Tuesday."

"Yeah, sure," I said. We did this a lot.

I went to the shower, let the water warm, and soaped up. I was not in the mood to wash my hair.

After a minute, I heard Olivia knock and enter, because you never want to sneak up on someone in the shower. Trust me, us hookers have plenty more horror stories about *that* than, like, bad butt sex. Anyhow, she says, "I'm dirty, too. Can I join you?"

I debated for a moment, because this might be her initiation for sex. I said, "It's been a long day with two sessions and stopping a robbery. I really just want a shower."

She slid aside the curtain, standing there nude with perky tits, and cocked her head and smiled. "Hey, that's fine. Let's soap up and go where we go. I'm cool with it."

I nodded. We soaped up. We've showered together for years, since high school. It is one of our favorite ways to spend time when we're in the mood to be close but not have sex, which seemed like what tonight was.

Mostly, she worked on me. Our relationship is, as one of my hooker friends, Cecilia, said once, "Interesting." From the start, Olivia initiated and was the aggressor in everything. One day, I'll tell you about that.

Anyhow, after I started being a hooker, I think subconsciously she felt a little threatened. And now . . . now she is the aggressor and initiates most of the time, but during the sex, she seeks to please me. She knows well what I like and is willing to give me sexual pleasure without any return, though I always will return if I'm able.

Her pet move is to go down and start licking my ass. Believe me, there is nothing like the feeling of a tongue up your butt.

So, I wait . . . I decide not to do anything and let her decide. If she's in the mood, I'll do it with her. If not, I'm going to bed.

She slowly soaps and I feel her go to her knees in the light water building in the shower She soaps my legs, down to my feet and up to my bottom. She gently cleans me.

Then I feel her tongue.

Then it's on.

At the ungodly time of 8:03 the next morning, the doorbell rings. I'm up to pee, but don't plan to stay up. I'm wearing yellow panties, nothing else, and feel like I'm hungover. I'm that tired. Olivia is still in bed out cold. She's snoring.

Now, the doorbell ringing can be nothing good. No one rings on the doorbell with good news. I figure it's a salesperson.

Then I heard a beep, and realize I got a text. I finish peeing, flush, throw on a gray terrycloth robe, and check my.

Uh oh.

OPEN THE DOOR. MEDINA.

I wince. Medina Kane is now the woman in charge of Special Operations, the government division that deals with the paranormal. I never joined Ops. Not my kind of thing, saving the world based on their rules and doing what they want. And I knew they'd never go with the hooker thing, but I gotta take care of myself. Sure, they say I make a great salary, but I've seen that go wrong many a time. Medina's only been in charge a couple months, but I met her for a lunch like a month ago. She's okay, y'know, but can be kind of bossy.

Anyhowwwwwwww . . . I had texted her last night about Charlie's gem, right before we fell asleep at 2:43. I assumed she was here to pick it up. Ops' headquarters was just across town.

And I looked like crap.

Racing to the door, I open it to find her.

Medina is like thirty, a pretty and charismatic woman — I've heard all Kanes are charismatic. Medina is a little chunky around the waist, but she hid that with fashionable clothes. Her blonde hair was very curly, parted in the middle and flat on top, held back with hairpins. She has wide-ass, bright blue eyes, and wears a lot of mascara and make-up. Her blush is light pink, and her lipstick is bright red. She wore a red blazer, white blouse, and black pants with matching heels. Her dress looked . . . official. Uh, oh.

"Uh, hi, Miss Kane."

"Medina. Can I come in?"

I move aside and she enters. I ask, "Anything to drink?"

"Coffee?"

"Not ready yet."

Medina smiled. "Just a water then."

We move to the kitchen. My kitchen is nice, but it is small. Stainless steel appliances, white upper cabinets and black lower cabinets with black and white checkerboard backsplash. Nothing fancy. I'm not into eating or cooking. I can't eat and gain weight, and men are around to buy me food when I want to eat.

Anyhow, I toss her a small Sparklets' bottle, which she catches defiantly. Uh, deftly. Then she sits and says, "I got the text. Where's the gem?"

"In the bedroom. I just got up. I was out late."

Medina studied me, then nodded. "Yes, I've seen footage of the Cube."

"Footage?"

"You're all over the news and internet, Cube."

"Uh, like I've said, I was asleep. And before that I had, uh, my, uh, girlfriend. Haven't seen anything."

Medina arched an eyebrow. "I really could care less if you were doing Jennifer Aniston last night. I *do* care about you running around like a third-rate Batgirl."

Her tone irritated me. She knew I was the Cube, of course. And she kind of protected me from the NSA and WSA and shit, because she liked me. But I'm not some idiot.

"Hey, I went to get some info, got it, and wanted a fucking pizza that a robber ruined. Don't bitch at me."

At that moment, Oliva entered, wearing nothing but a white nightshirt that just barely covered her privates. She had sleep in her eyes and looked a mess.

"Ah, the magician," said Medina. "Nice to see you, Olivia."

Olivia glared at her, looked at me, then said, "I'm going back to bed. It's too early in the morning for government shit."

Medina ignored her. "I'm not here to cause trouble, Shelby. I like you. Can you just get me the gem? Then I'll be long gone."

"Sure. Did you give me access to the app?"

"Yep. Just download the link I texted you."

"Thanks."

"Don't abuse it," she said, shaking a finger.

I gave her the middle-finger salute, she laughed, and I went to my bedroom. I quickly retrieved the gem and passed it to her.

She smiled and said, "I appreciate it. I just don't want you to get hurt."

"You're not my mother."

Medina rolled her eyes. "Thank God." Then she laughed. "Take some time today and watch yourself."

"No thanks."

I showed her the door and was glad when she was gone. I like her, but she makes me nervous.

After Medina left, Olivia returned. She'd combed her hair, but hadn't done much else, though she now looked alert. "What was that about?"

"Annoying bullshit," I said. "I gave her the gem. I don't need it, and it's probably dangerous, and it will keep her away from the warehouse Charlie referred to. I don't want her in my way. Davis is *mine*."

Olivia said seriously, "I'm with you there."

She looked hot standing there in my shirt, her hip jutting out. I moved forward and said, "Nice of you to run away."

She smiled. "I didn't want to get on her bad side. She doesn't like me."

"She doesn't like me either. She's a control freak."

Now, I'll admit, I was turned on. I'd woken up and knew Olivia would be gone for a few days. I stepped forward and rubbed the back of her hair and gave a little tug to tip her head back.

"Oh?" she asked. "I can be like that, too, especially when I want some satisfaction."

I batted her eyelashes coyly and said, "Oh, *really*?"

She reached with her right hand and caressed my butt. "Get into bed and I'll show you what us control freaks do."

"Damn, that was good," said Olivia as she exited the shower later. I had already showered and put on black track pants with a white stripe and a light green T-shirt. She toweled off.

"I know, it was. We're pretty good when we get into it."

She approached me, for I was sitting on the bed painting my toenails pink. As she kissed my cheek, she whispered, "We don't do this enough."

"I agree."

Then she sighed. "Sadly, tonight's the last night until Sunday, when I'll be back from Tahoe. Tomorrow is a train wreck."

I wiggled my toes and said, "It's okay, baby. You're my friend. Always."

"I know. I love you."

"I love you, too," I said, and I did, but not in that sort of way. We just loved each other and were bonded in ways other people could never be . . . maybe like solider buddies in a big war or something? I dunno. But it was unique, and always would be.

She suddenly snapped her fingers. "Look, no more dodging the elephant in the room. We need to figure out what to do about Woody. I can't take him with me to Tahoe, knowing he's really not a marionette, and if I leave him alone, God knows what he'll get into."

"Are you rehearsing there today?"

She shook her head. "No, tomorrow. Today I have to deal with the plumbing at the condo."

"Oh, yeah, I forgot your pipe problem. Okay. Well, I'm on call from noon to eight today, so tomorrow we make our move, because I, the brilliant Cube, have a plan. A trap."

She rolled her eyes. "With you in charge of the trap, we'll probably both wind up in giant nets like cartoon characters."

I gave her the finger.

Chapter Four
Setting the Trap

The difficulty with setting a trap for Woody was that his mysterious stalking appearances were seemingly irregular. But I wasn't stupid. I had figured out one consistency to his appearance, and we were counting on that Monday night.

We discussed my plan on the drive to the Magic House on Monday night as she prepped for a rehearsal run. I was tired. Monday was kickboxing in the morning, and I'd been on call from 12-4. Nothing major, a quick fuck for two grand, hardly worth my time.

Anyhow, the walkthrough was something she normally did, just a walk through before a road trip — you know, like football teams do. I sat in the first row, wearing white pants and a red and white striped shirt with tennis shoes. She was in semi-costume, wearing the black bodice and nude hose with over-the-knee red boots and her white jacket, but no hat or jewelry. It was hot under the lights, but she had to wear the jacket — magicians relied on puling things out of their sleeves.

As she walked around the stage studying it, she told me, "You're lucky to see all of this, you know. Most people have no clue how much these entertainment shows are organized and detailed. You can't just wander around the stage at random. You have to stay under the lights, not block certain sviews, not hit hidden props or doors on the stage, and be in the right place at the right time every time — all the while looking sexy and attractive."

"I know that shit, and believe me, you've got that last part down," I said with a smile.

"Flattery is appreciated. But the point is, this is hard work, and this stupid stalker doll is making me nervous. Thank God he's not part of my act yet. But, anyhow, if I make a mistake at the wrong time, and I'll wind up with a sword stuck in my gut or something."

"Don't worry. We'll take care of him," I said confidently.

She paused and looked at me with obvious anxiety. "You're sure we have to do it here?"

"I'm sure this place is the key connection," I said. "Woody has never stalked you at home. You've found him in various areas in the building here, and the one time you found him in your car, it was in the parking lot here when you came out after a show."

"That seems like circumstantial evidence."

"I could do some better detective work, but it's much easier and much more fun to set a trap."

She glared at me, pausing before a set stop at the water tank. "Fun for you. Not me! I don't want to wind up with a knife in my back!"

I rolled my eyes. "Oh, you *do* carry on!"

After that, she concentrated on her act. She was good. Not perfect, but good. The average person wouldn't catch her mistakes. I caught them because I know her act so well.

Just after nine, I felt a ping from the app Medina had provided, so I rose, stretched, then said, "I'm beat. You gonna quit soon?"

"I have to run the second half of the act again. I had seven errors," she said, using our preplanned code that told me she was ready.

"Okay. You do that. I'll see you at home. Want me to wait up?"

"Nah. I'll be fine."

"Okay. Love you. Be safe."

I walked out. But I didn't leave. Once I got to the backstage door, I knew where Woody was thanks to my app. The app Medina got me could lock onto a paranormal aura, and Woody's was distinctive. Moreover, he wasn't trying to hide it. He was trying to scare Olivia.

I had figured out no one was fucking with her mind. I knew Woody had an aura. Logically, he was doing this on his own. Another reason he could only stalk her on the grounds of the Magic House. She had never taken him home with her.

Why he was doing this, I had no God damn fucking idea. But once we caught him, we'd put a drill up his ass to get him to talk. The trick was that I wasn't sure precisely *what* paranormal ability he had, and therefore I wasn't positive how to stop him. But I did have a plan.

I moved quickly up the ladder into the wings over the stage where Olivia continued to run her act. She as soaked in perspiration. I didn't see that from the seats, but this close, it was obvious. She'd been working hard. And she was scared. And it was kind of hot. Sexy hot, I mean. Not for the first time, I wondered how I got so lucky to have such a good friend.

Well, my being willing to hunt a stalking puppet was probably one of the many factors in our friendship being so strong.

Marionette, I mean. Fuck. I never get that right.

Anyhow, I waited and watched the app. It was like watching a video game waiting to strike. He was moving through the air ducts, and when he reached one backstage, he paused. He obviously was watching Olivia.

Then he pushed aside the grate, which was open, so he'd preplanned this. He had to have been *outside* the grate to unscrew it.

Once he was out, he was about fifteen feet behind Olivia, in an area with a bunch of trunks and a portable wardrobe. He moved to open the trunk.

That's when I swung down like fucking Batgirl on a rope.

He looked up and shouted, "No, wait!"

Before he could say anything else or even move, I kicked him in the head and he flew like a fucking field goal in the Super Bowl, or whatever that is they play. He hit the backstage curtain and dropped like a rock to the floor.

"You got him!" shrieked Olivia, as if she'd just gotten engaged.

"Yeah, but let's make sure he can't get away. Then we can talk to his fucking wood-fuck ass."

"You got it."

Olivia and I worked quickly to secure Woody. Fortunately, the one advantage of being a magician was having plenty of restraint devices around for magic tricks. We took him backstage, behind the red curtain and a fake wall, to what looked like a big storage area. It was full of crates, dusty, and windowless. The floorboard was ancient but clean and well maintained. Perfect.

We used the pillory part of a guillotine used for the old 'chop off her head but she's alive' trick to secure Woody. Then we used a chain and one of many winches backstage to lift him up, putting us eye-to-eye, so to speak. Our timing was perfect. Just as Olivia cuffed his hands behind his back, he began to come around.

Standing before him, I folded my arms over my chest and said loudly to Olivia, who stood on my left, "So how do we get this piece of woodlice to talk? We can't exactly waterboard a puppet. Marionette. Whatever."

Olivia folded her arms over her chest as well and glared at Woody. "I dunno."

I snapped my fingers. "Hell, we don't need water. He's made of wood and a bunch of flammable preservatives, right? Find me a lighter."

"Hey! Hey! *None of that*! What are you, savages?" he squeaked, struggling in his restraints.

I flicked him on the forehead with a finger, like a teenage bully, and said, "You're the stalker, puppet!"

"Marionette!"

"Whatever!" Olivia and I both shouted back at the same time.

"I *wasn't* stalking her," said Woody, and he winked his left eye at me.

"Then what were you doing?" I asked, cocking my head.

"I was using her to get to you, obviously!" he shouted, clearly exasperated. "If you hadn't been so busy knocking me out, I would have explained I was trying to find you to help you!"

"Me?" I asked. "I'm just hooker."

"Don't blow snow up my ass, babe. You're the Cube."

Eager to change the subject, I went on the attack. "Why stalk her?"

"*She's* easy to find. She's a famous magician. You're *not*," he said, clearly making a dig at my rather erratic super-hero career.

I ignored the insult. "What, you couldn't afford to schedule me through the agency?"

He looked surprised. "I never thought of it, actually."

"It's just as well," I said. "Puppets don't bring in enough bucks for a high-class call girl." I saw Olivia smile at that one.

"It ain't like a got a woody to satisfy, so it didn't occur to me! What do you think I'd get from you, a good sanding?"

"I do spankings."

"Whatever. Besides, I'm not even real! You try getting a VISA when you look like this!"

"Okay, knock it off, you two. This is not the fifth grade," said Olivia. "Let's say we believe your rather unbelievable story for a moment. I mean, I have heard some stranger things."

I looked at her. "Really?"

"Well, no. But let's go with it. How do you expect to help my friend?" Olivia asked Woody.

Woody looked at me. "Kids, there's a cost for using your powers, and you're both using 'em recklessly."

"Cost?"

He rolled his eyes, quite a feat for a puppet. Marionette. Whatever. He looked at me and asked, "Kid, what shit-ass cult trained you? Don't you know *anything*?" Then he looked at Olivia. "And you, magician, I gotta know, what necromancer trained you? Because they need their license pulled."

"License?" asked Olivia.

Ignoring her, I said, "I wasn't in a cult, pine-head. I'm an elemental channeler."

Olivia said, "And I wasn't trained. I learned necromancy after I killed my dad and tried to bring him back to life."

He looked at me, then Olivia, then back at me, then at Olivia and said, "And you think *my* story is crazy!"

"What is the cost?" asked Olivia, taking the words out of my mouth.

He didn't answer directly. First, he looked at me and said, "Kid, you're not just an elemental channeler. You're using necromancy, too. You're drawing on cutie's power here, subconsciously of course, which makes you much more powerful when she's around."

"I don't use necromancy," I said confidently.

He looked at Olivia and said, "Shut it, blondie. Olivia. You use necromancy. What does that *mean*? Communicating with the dead and using magic based on the dead has a lotta variations."

"I channel the aura of the dead if they are recently expired, and I can manipulate the dead, including zombies. What else does a necromancer do?"

He looked at me. "You tell me. What do you do?"

I studied him. I wasn't sure how much I should discuss how my powers worked. You do that, and next thing you know some asswipe teenager posts it on the internet, and then everyone knows what you do and how to kick your ass. Still . . . ah, fuck it. if I was the cautious type, I wouldn't be a call girl *or* a superheroine.

"I channel earth, air, wind, and fire. I've never done anything with the dead."

He turned to Olivia. "She doesn't realize there's more to it than that, but you do, don't you?"

Looking a little guilty, Olivia nodded once and said, "I get energy from the dead. I can use it to channel force, kind of like strong wind but without wind. I can also focus on the body of a person and reverse channel to draw out the life force of certain organs."

"From which dead do you get the energy?"

I looked at Olivia. She shrugged and said, "I don't know what he means. He's not my puppet."

"If you call me a puppet again, I'm gonna forget all this and go home," muttered Woody.

"Just answer the question," I said wearily. My back hurt from standing around looking tough on a wooden floor in bad shoes.

"Well, when you draw from the dead, you're taking energy from those dead souls. Who they are has an effect on the terms of the usage."

"Terms?"

He shook his head and clucked his tongue. "Mannnnnnnnn . . . your dumb stories must be true, because you two don't know shit."

"I know shit, and it's right between your ears," I snapped back.

"Drawing on the dead has consequences. Terms. Think of it . . . think of magic like a bank. You pull power out, your reserves run low. You gotta put in to take out."

Frowning, I asked, "What do I put in and where? Us hookers are used to getting it the other way around."

"That's the big question. It depends who you're drawing power from." He looked at Olivia. "You don't get any sense of anyone you know?"

She frowned. "No . . . I feel this buzz in my head, and then zap! It's not like a conversation."

"Okay, we can figure this out. That's where I can help you. My sect wants me to train you, blondie, but obviously I gotta train *both* of you lame-asses."

"I'm not being trained by a puppet. Marionette. Whatever," I snapped, rolling my eyes.

He gave a labored sigh and said, "Then you'll be dead within a few weeks."

I looked at Olivia. "He doesn't know shit. He was up to something, probably some fuck-ass worshipper from a cult, and we caught him and now he's coming up with shit to save his stiff ass. Let's just find some gasoline and be done with this. I have dinner reservations."

"No, listen to me! Look, my sect, we need you to be a better fighter because our sect is in danger. In return, we can tell you how to find Davis, and I know you hate him for the kidnapping. And he's still loose and is into some major shit. But unless you're ready, he'll wipe the floor with you."

Well, thanks to Charlie Saturday night, I knew where Davis was, but the fact that this idiot made of wood knew about Davis and what he did to me angered me, and I couldn't discount he might have more information than Charlie, info I could use. I was pissed. Menacingly, I stepped forward and put my right hand on his head and pushed. He yelped as I said, "Don't toy with me, puppet! Where is Davis?"

"Easy, blondie, easy!"

I lessened the pressure, but kept my hand in place and said, "I can channel ice through you and shatter you. I guess you're some sort of zombie, so you might *think* since you're not alive I can't do anything to make you suffer. But you *have* an aura. I can sense it. Somewhere inside, you're human. You can die."

"Please, blondie."

"Talk."

Olivia put a gentle hand on my left shoulder from behind to make sure I was under control. Then she said to Woody, "You better talk fast. Since I can't throw your stalking ass in jail, I'm getting a lighter if I don't like your explanation."

I found a lighter on the table and held it up with a smile.

"Davis is a torture magician, but he was trained by the man that runs a cult that tried to gain power by wiping out our sect. His name is Flannagan. We want him," he said very quickly.

"What is your sect?" I asked.

"We've part of ZUN, the Zombie Unified Nation. But we're a sub-section. We're souls that should be zombies, but through some weird totem influence, we wound up with souls in animations: puppets, marionettes, toys, dolls. You're right, sweet butt, I am technically a zombie. But I'm not dumb like your typical zombie."

"How many are there of you?" asked Olivia.

He winced. "Uh, our files are confidential."

I flicked the lighter and smiled.

"Fine! Whatever! You're a bully. Are you a dom at the agency?"

"Nope."

"Whatever. Our sect is down to just a couple dozen. And I want to find my sister, Leanna. The last I saw, before the cult broke us up, she was a rag-doll in a circus somewhere in the Midwest."

I looked at Olivia. "What do you think?"

"Let's talk privately."

We moved to the other side of the room, where we could still see Woody but where he couldn't hear us. I said, "Some of his story rings true, some doesn't make sense. What should we do?"

"It's your super-hero career," said Olivia. "I don't trust him. He hid in my dressing room!"

"Oh, get over it. You've had worse things see you naked and you know it!"

She rolled her eyes. "Now that's just not nice, especially coming from a lady of the night."

I winked. "Aw, I was just sassing you." I looked at Woody. "I don't trust him. I think we should keep him in a box somewhere until you get back from Tahoe."

"I know about ZUN, Shelby. They're really powerful. They might be up to something else, or he might be rebelling form them, but they're not someone to cross on a whim."

I nodded. "I know. But I don't know what else to do."

She glared at him. "Neither do I. He's on my shit list anyhow for stalking me." She looked back at me. "Okay. Let's shove him in a box and you lock him up in our storage locker."

We shared a storage locker at Extra Space Storage over on Oakey. Olivia obviously had a lot of props and shit, and I had a ton of clothes. The storage locker was overflow, because even with my portable storage at the condo, I needed more. It worked out for both of us.

"Right. I'm on it."

We approached Woody. I said, "She has an act in Tahoe this week."

"I know. I'm part of the act, remember? Man, maybe blondes *are* dumb."

Ignoring his insult, I said, "You are going into our storage locker until she gets back and I can check some things out."

Surprising me, he didn't throw a fit or resist. All he did was ask, "Can I have a bunch of books?"

"Whatever you want."

"Brad Thor will work. I just got into his stuff. But mostly, well, I like the classics. Like <u>Moby Dick</u>."

I rolled my eyes. "Fine. We're gonna let you out, stuff you in that red storage container over there, and take you to your new home. It's low rent."

"Fine. Whatever. But when the Tahoe act is over, we gotta get on this. Davis moves around a lot, and our sect is in danger every day."

Olivia said, "I've made a commitment. I'll help, unless Shelby decides you're a liar."

"All the truth, cross my heart and promise to die," he said.

"That'd be more convincing if you weren't already dead," I muttered.

Twenty-six minutes later, we exited the storage locker and set the security, both physical and aural, just before the 10 P.M. closing time. I got in the passenger side, and Olivia started up her Stinger as she said, "What do you think?"

"Seeing if he says put is the main test. I'm going to follow up on Charlie's info. In between, I'll fuck for money and see what I can dig up."

"Okay. I wish I weren't going."

I rubbed her cheek. "This is your career, your life. Go and have fun. Wow the dumpheads of Tahoe."

She smiled. "Okay. If you insist."

"I do. You have a career. Me, I just have a fucking job." I laughed. "Literally."

Chapter Five Davis
Stakeout

Olivia was nervous when I took her to the airport Tuesday morning, the thirtieth. When possible, I tried to do this, because it's often our best chance to talk. Tuesday, I had to, because I knew she was worried. She didn't say much. When she left, we kissed, and she mumbled something about making sure asshole didn't break out of storage.

But Woody was far from my biggest concern Tuesday. I was almost relieved when Olivia was gone, because now I could focus on checking out the warehouse and finding out about Davis before going on-call.

By now, you know I hate him. I'll get into details a bit later, but right now, I have a job to focus on. And this being March in Vegas, it's hot. Actually, March isn't so bad, if you're in the shade.

Of course, I'm going to be on a rooftop in the sun in mid-day.

Great.

Now, hookers and super-heroes are, by nature, creatures of action. But like I've said, the talking is the hidden skill of hooking, and the searching is the hidden skill of the superheroine. Sure, I got my start by punching out someone at Chevron and, okay, just the other night I told you about the throwdown at Domino's. But those are the exceptions. A lot of work goes into finding contacts like Charlie and hunting down and preparing a trap . . . just like we did for Woody at the Magic House. I gotta do the same for Davis. It will take several days, maybe even a couple of weeks, to properly scout the place and be prepared to take him on.

My agency knows men like outfits, so they have a preferred costumer, and we get dirt-cheap rates. I stop by and rent a gray plumber's uniform, complete with a blue baseball cap. The guy really looks, and I finally say, "Hey, I just fuck 'em, I don't comment on their fantasies."

However, this was not for hooking. This was for Davis.

At 1:45 that afternoon, I was on the roof of one of several buildings near Davis' alleged warehouse. I had parked at a parking garage, then walked a few blocks to Ed's Flooring, which is logically a flooring warehouse.

Now, general rule, gang, anywhere you go you are on CCTV. But that's not an absolute. For one thing, companies don't always do CCTV on the roof because birds and animals set off motion sensors and the heat in Vegas can do weird things to heat-sensing apps. And if you have a store where the goods aren't cash and carry, it's really an expense the business just doesn't need.

Ed's is like that. I mean, who is going to pop in from the roof and try to haul away marble tile? It's not like you can stuff samples in your pockets. And flooring costs a fucking fortune. You don't walk in and pay for it like a cheeseburger. Almost all the business here, even from non-hookers, is internet or credit card, so there's no cash on hand.

The furniture warehouse is long and narrow, a block east of Davis' warehouse, and about ten feet taller. Perfect. I scale a maintenance ladder next to a bed of cacti, completely ignored by the three customers and one salesperson inside. The first floor is all the flooring. The second floor is office space.

Once on the roof, I use binoculars I bought at a spy store. Now, another tip, you can go stalker on anyone with a few bucks and a little internet shopping. Now, if you go stalker and get in trouble, that makes you really easy for the cops to trace. I don't have that problem. Crooks don't call the cops on you, they just try to decapitate you. Or rape you and then decapitate you. . . sometimes not always in that order. Anyhow, I'm not recommending this. It's just a tip in case, say, some Russian spy moves into your condo next door.

The roof has several air conditioning ports and vents. I have my pick of seven fully secure spots. I pick the one with the best view. This area also has a full metal screen around the a/c unit, which is idea for setting up my portable camera.

I needed to see the place in person the first time, because I need an idea of what I'm looking at on the video. You'd be amazed what shadows and other shit can do to video.

Davis' warehouse faces the opposite road. The small road between the furniture store and Davis is an access road for delivery trucks to both places. The stores are butt-to-butt.

The back of the warehouse has a dock, sort of like you'd see at a mid-sized post office. There's two ramps on each side, stairs, and mostly the docking bay is the height for big rigs to back up to the dock. Typical shit. But they didn't have any trucks present. They do have two forklifts, which are moving around crates, as if to position them for a later pickup.

The warehouse is in decent shape. It's surrounded by chain-link fencing with barb wire and obvious security gates. I'm sure it's loaded with other detectors, but they aren't going to see me on the roof next door.

I set up my camera and get ready to leave, when suddenly I hear the roar of a sports car. I pause, and a yellow Maserati pulls into the parking lot. That can only be one person.

Davis.

The Maserati parks near the forklift operator and Davis jumps out. He's six-three, 250, bald, about thirty-five. He has tiny eyes, big ears, and a perpetually mean look. He's wearing a total douche bag outfit of a white sports shirt, red pants, and a lot of jewelry.

I begin to feel a blinding rage as I see him. People talk about this . . . and it's true. Olivia says it's from adrenaline. Maybe. I think it's just pure, good old-fashioned hate.

But I stay cool. He's too far away to make any reliable strike. He gets out and is only there for ten minutes, most of which is spent shouting at the forklift operators and clearly making them feel like dogshit.

Which is how he made me feel the day he kidnapped me.

First off, disclaimer, I wasn't kidnapped long. I was only kidnapped for like thirty minutes. Still, it fucking counts. It's like, there's no being a little bit pregnant. There's no being a little bit kidnapped.

As I think I mentioned, this happened on March 27, 2020. I had been out on a call until four in the morning. I got breakfast. I needed some tampons as that time of the month was coming, and more urgently some Advil. I was tired and in a bad mood. I had put in a lot of work and not cleared all that much, just a couple thousand.

I stopped at the Kroeger off Sahara. Trust me, every lady of the night knows every drug and grocery store in town. You always need to be ready for emergencies, lie you're in a hurry and bring the wrong purse, or suddenly have gas and it's a backdoor night.

I was tired. It was about six in the morning and there was just one checker and some lady paying with a card that had expired. Are you kidding me? I finally got through the line and dragged my ass outta there. I get to my car. I pull out and this black work van, like some sort of 90s Dodge, blows through a stop sign and nearly hits me.

I throw my window down and flip him off and shout, "Fuckhole!"

Then I go and turn left to head for the other end of the parking lot when the douche bag comes around again.

He blocks my path. Now I'm pissed.

I get out of the car, planning to channel earth and hurl some bricks from a nearby planter into his face. "You fuck, you messed with the wrong woman this morning!"

Just as I went to channel, he flipped the ground from under me telekinetically, and I fell on my ass. He grabbed my hair and slammed my face into the side of my car. That hurt.

The he had me in handcuffs before I knew what the fuck was going on. And he flipped me over his shoulder and tossed me in the back of the van. I kicked at him, but I had no leverage. The van was full of old carpets and had a custom rail bar. He quickly flipped a chain around the cuffs and rail bar, and suddenly I was his prisoner.

He slammed the door shut.

Just like that.

I was scared shitless. He could channel, obviously. Did he know I could? Not if my aural blockers were working, and they should have been. I knew I sure as shit wasn't tired anymore. I was ready to wet myself.

There was a solid wall between me and the cab. The entire inside was black, other than the carpets. It was like being in a steel cage.

I tested my channeling. I had powers, so he didn't have aural suppressors in the van. I hoped that held true.

Part of me just couldn't believe this shit was happening. How could I get kidnapped? I was a fucking superheroine!

How embarrassing.

And frightening.

The chains and cuffs were going to hold, unless I channeled earth and crashed the van. That carried a lot of risk. But if I let him take me back to his place, whatever the fuck that was, he could drug me or shoot me before I could do anything. I'd have to act in a split second and knocks his ass out. And hope he didn't have friends.

Then it hit me. Olivia had told me how to escape handcuffs many times, because trick ones weren't reliable for the stage. Break the thumbs, which are really lots of little bones, the proper way. She knew how to do it. I didn't, but I could channel earth. Could I focus that on my own bones?

I had to try.

I gritted my teeth and channeled and felt the left one break. Motherfucker, it hurt, but I could cry in pain and idiot-fuck douche bag up front would just think I as some scared blonde bimbo.

I realized I didn't have to break the right one. I could just slide free now, because the chain to the rail wasn't secured to the cuffs in any way, just looped through. Once my left hand was free, I could pull the right free.

But I didn't. I sat there like a big pussy, crying, putting on a good act in case he had the van wired. Sicko pervs like to do that sort of thing.

We drove a while. I mean, we had to be on the outskirts of the general metro area. I didn't know where the fuck we were, though I later found out we were in an old neighborhood in North Las Vegas — that's the city, not the northern part of Vegas. We weren't too far from Nellis Air Force Base.

When we parked, I braced myself. I was ready. My channeling was strong.

He opened the door and had a gun, but I was ready. Once the van door was open, I had access to enough space to channel a strong wind. I channeled wind and earth, blowing the gun away from me and rupturing the concrete of a garage floor beneath him. He flew up in the air, and I slipped the chain and jumped out at him.

I landed on his chest and knocked the gun from his hand with my left hand, but that caused my broken thumb to impact the metal and I screamed like a motherfucker. He then punched me in the face and flung me off him, both bodily and by channeling wind.

Hitting a pile of cartons, I was stunned. If he pushed his attack, he had me. But he didn't, the gutless shit. He ran.

I tried to chase him, but we were in some type of warehouse district. Everything was a maze. I lost him in a hurry.

Racing back to the van, I called the cops. They needed to process the scene, and I needed free medical care to get my thumb fixed. I wasn't paying for that shit myself, and crime victims have a fund in Nevada. These are the things you learn from fellow hookers who have been beaten up.

Anyhow, it made for a very long fucking morning after a long fucking night. I called in sick two days. It's the only time I ever missed two straight days of work. I told Nina what happened. She's my boss and needed to know. And I told Olivia, of course. They were the only ones that knew.

The cops found nothing, but Davis had a record and obviously his prints were all over the van. It was registered to a fake corporation.

The warehouse was owned by a company that was based in Japan. They didn't know Davis at all. Why he took me there was a mystery we never solved.

But I did find out Davis was a major totem fuck and paranormal player. Taking him down would feel good, personally and professionally.

As I watched the fuck, I realized I was going on-call. I had to put my anger aside. I forced myself to stay calm, focus on breathing.

He didn't stay long. I was about to leave, but he left as well. There was no fucking way I could follow his Maserati in my car, which is a fine piece of machinery, but let's face it, tailing a Maserati is probably only possible in a Maserati.

But now I knew he was there.

And I knew soon his ass would be mine.

From three to eleven on Tuesday, I'm on call. Now, as I've said, I'm ranked fairly high in the agency these days, and I have made good cash the last five years. I also don't blow my cash up my nose or veins. I try to limit myself to three calls a day.

Sounds like a lot? Not really. Some girls, the new girls who really want to score, they'll do like seven or eight calls in an eight-hour shift and do a thirty-minute minimum. And trust me, on a Friday or a Saturday, they stay fully booked and make more money than a fucking printing press. How they do it, I dunno. If I got fucked that much two days in a row, I wouldn't be able to walk for a week. But if you're desperate for money, you'll do it.

That's not so much the norm for our agency, the Empire. Nina is a really efficient madam. In eight hours, we're limited to four calls and a one-hour minimum. Logically, that's hard to do sometimes. Vegas is pretty connected along the Strip, but we have lots of private clients and business clients who have us drag out to North LV or Henderson. One fuck even had me go to Utah for a day to fuck him at his software corporation. I declined, though. Other states, except California, are weird. This is what Olivia says. Hell, my trip to New Mexico convinced me of that.

See, Vegas has a simple hands-off approach to prostitution. Technically, it's illegal, but that's just to keep streetwalkers off the strip. Or to bring you in and hold you if you're nuts or coked out of your mind or something. Like any large city in America, it's perfectly condoned by those in charge because it's part of, ah, tourism.

Nutcase places like Utah and North Dakota, probably, shit places like that, you never know. I have no desire to spend a night in jail.

Anyhow, being the Cube, I have to be more flexible with my hours than some. I like daytime hours when I can get them. A lot of the girls have kids and can't do days, while I have to be able to hunt down leads as the Cube some nights or go to one of Olivia's magic shows, and I need evenings.

You might think days are dead, and sure three to eleven, those are fairly early hours, but you'd be surprised sometimes. Some guys like an early call and then take you to dinner. Those are the talkers.

Have I explained the three types I get at my agency? I have my own names for them.

One is the *professional*. This is your rich guy who is a businessman too busy to date, or some guy having an affair. This is strictly wham-bam-thank-you-ma'am, turn over the cash, and really it's over after fifteen or twenty minutes and they don't usually keep you around once they've had their happy moment. They don't haggle, it's all a pure business transaction. Most of them are polite, but they aren't personal. We're just an object, a way of stroking their dick and ego, because most of them could never get a girl as hot as me on their own.

The second is the *talker*. This is the guy who is really just lonely. A lot of them don't even get much into the sex. They just need to unload about their fat wife, their ugly girlfriend, their terrible job, you know, everything wrong in their life, most of which is their own fault. I mean, really, if your life sucks, change it, don't go complain to a hooker.

The last is the *power-tripper*. These are the guys we hookers have to watch out for. Think Putin on a bad day. They're there to exert power over you, they want control. They're acting out on me because they hate their mother or wife or girlfriend or, more often than not, life in general. You know, nutbags. Some are dangerous, though I have to say, the agency screens very well and I've only had a couple of these types that made me really want to leave the room — not that I have to. I just channel and rock their world. Anyhow, they get off on having property. We're just an object to them, something to unload their anger and insecurities on. They suck. And these are the ones that, if you cross them somehow, they can get violent.

I got a call at about four to be on location at five. That fee you pay up front gets split between me and the house, but the appointment booker gets fifteen percent off the top. The tips theoretically all go to me, but the agency I work for is high class. They run credit. They knew what the guy can afford. I have a minimum set to clear of one grand per appointment for the house. Now, I don't give out anything for free. I wouldn't anyhow. But knowing this, I know I have to make two to make anything worth my while.

There are occasional exceptions. I had a guy once who had his legs shot off in Iraq. I looked him up and verified it. I did him for free and ate the grand. I also did him for free outside the agency twice, but then he moved to Seattle. I had one real hot woman businessman who just made me wet looking at her. She was like . . . hot. She was a closet lesbian and offered me ten grand. And I . . . and I *don't* know why . . . but I turned it down. I think because she seemed so desperate, and I wanted her to know there was nothing wrong with liking girls. I told her I'd do her for free if she'd just admit she likes girls. And she did. Anyhow, a week later I got a box with the ten grand in hundred-dollar bills anyhow, so maybe that doesn't count. She never asked for me again. I guess she couldn't face who she was.

Thank God I don't have that problem.

Anyhow, I'm off to the Bellagio for a five o'clock. At this point, I'm in a good mood. Client seems okay. Al Lenzini, a businessman from Milwaukee out here on vacation. Has good credit, but a first-timer with the agency. Nina likes one of us experienced girls with first-timers with good credit because she knows we'll let them think they got a deal with they didn't and turn 'em into repeat customers.

He had good credit. I'm thinking six grand for a full fuck, three if he just wants to talk or a hand-job or something. Somewhere in the middle for a BJ.

I'm wearing a white skirt and a blue button-down blouse with white swirls on it, white booties, and a blue hairband. I look cute, like a co-ed, as Nina thought that might be what he wants.

At room 717, I knock, and he quickly answers.

"Hi, I'm Shelby. Are you Al?" I ask, extending my hand.

Before me is a guy who has gotta be fifty with, of course, a belly on him, little muscle definition, and a tired, worn-out look. He had curly black hair, a big nose, and brown eyes. He's wearing a white shirt with a Green Bay Packers football team logo on it and jeans.

He shakes my hand. "Sure am. You're cute. Come on in."

"Thanks, you're pretty handsome yourself," I said with a winning smile and perfect teeth. I have a white purse over my shoulder, a small one. "Are we alone?"

"Yes. Come in, please," he says, gesturing to yet another dull looking, single-bed hotel room. I swear, when I go to Hell, I'll be trapped in a hotel where all the rooms look the same and I never escape.

"I have to check in, okay?"

"Sure," he says, and he sits on the bed. I sit at the table in a very poorly cushioned chair. I call in and say, "It's Shelby, I'm here."

Once she confirms, I hang up and turn to Al. "You in town for business?"

"Vacation. I'm divorced, kid is 26 and lives in Boston. I run a software company. We design software for small businesses. I do okay."

I nodded. "Sure. I guess you want to cut loose a little?" I ask, arching an eyebrow.

He reaches under the pillow and pulls out $300. "Here's what I have."

Immediately, I'm annoyed. This is not 1996. But he doesn't see that. I just smile and say sweetly, "Oh, honey, for $300 I won't even take off my shirt. Add a zero behind it and we have something."

He shrugs. "Business hasn't been too good, and my ex-wife takes everything."

I nod. He slumps, and I make him for a talker. He's miserable and his vacation has probably sucked, and he's probably at the end of it and is realizing he's going back to Milwaukee with the same fat belly and just as broke.

"Hey, it's okay, Al. I can work with, you know, two?"

Suddenly, something in him changes. He smirks and his eyes are suddenly lit up. "Oh?"

"Yeah, sure," I say, not liking the change in his body language.

He reaches under the pillow and pulls out five thousand. I smile, but I'm worried. What's this about?

"I'm surprised. You're a pretty nice whore. Most of you have a price a lot higher. You can have five, but we do things my way."

Instantly, I realize I missed on him, he's not a talker, he's a power-player. The best way to deal with them is feel out what they want.

"Hey, that's fine, baby, but I don't do a few things."

He unzipped his pants and removed a very hard member. "You're going to take off your clothes and lick my shoes while I jack off. And when I cum on them, you're going to lick them off."

I have only a split-second to decide without pissing him off. He's one of those power-trippers that wants to degrade and humiliate women. The five grand is a good enticement.

There comes a time in any profession when you have to swallow your pride and eat shit. I mean, not literally. But Olivia's been through this. Her ass has been pinched more times than the fruit at Kroeger's. At some point, you do what the boss wants.

I smile as if he gave me a gift and say seductively, "Do you want me clothed or nude?"

"Take 'em off. And I keep the panties."

"Sure," I say. Trophies aren't unusual for power-trippers.

I take the cash and put it in my purse. Always get the cash first. Always. Then I strip and don't mess around much. Once I'm nude, he snaps his fingers as he stands up and points at his shoes.

"On your knees, not your belly."

I kneel before him, woman before the throne of man — this is the sort of shit Olivia says all the time — and put my tongue on the tip of his shoe. It's one of those composites, dress shoes with rubber soles so they're comfortable.

"Ahhhhhhh. Ah, you're a sick whore, aren't you?" he says, stroking himself.

"Yes, sir," I say, because they all like it when you say that. It doesn't bother me. They're just words.

Really. Just words.

Licking his shoes is not fun, but I've done worse. I can tell by his grunts he's not going to last long.

"Move back!" he suddenly shouts.

I slide back and he lets go, angling his ejaculate to land on his shoes, at least for the most part. White goo covers them, and a couple spots on the floor.

"Lick 'em clean, whore."

I take a breath and start eating his cum. Now, male goop, it has the same sort of general taste, sort of slaty and sticky, but it can vary depending on diet and the man. His is super-salty.

Eating cum is not really my thing. Some girls really get into it. I could get into it if it was my man, but this guy is an asshole. Eating it in this case is basically like taking terrible medicine. Just do it, swallow it, and don't think about it.

Once his shoes are clean, I look up at him and smile. "You taste good."

"Yeah, you just like it all. How much cum do you eat?"

I stand up and slide back. "You know, not all that much. You're different, though. You're worth of it."

I know, you want to gag, but you gotta play to the ego of a power-player or you wind up broke and locked in a car trunk somewhere, or missing some teeth.

He smiles. "Get the fuck out of here, you dirty tramp."
I wink and say, "Enjoy the panties."
I am very fucking glad to leave that place.

After calling the service to check out and let them know the type of guy Al was, I get in the car and drive home, far too fast. I'm pissed. No one likes humiliation. Even those bondage slut girls that claim it gets them off don't really want it. They would much rather be at home with Mister Right watching Netflix and eating chocolate than be buck naked getting whipped on the ass.

I stop at JIB (that's Jack-in-the Box for you non-Westerners) and get a soda. I want to brush my teeth, but I can't even wait twenty minutes to get home.

Once I have the soda, I feel a little better, but I still feel dirty. Still . . . I have cleared a couple grand, so that's not bad for what amounted to about twenty minutes of actual time in the room. What's a little degradation for that kind of cash? I know people that sell themselves out for a lot less. Like stockriders and bankers. Stockbrokers, I mean.

Anyhow, I'm mostly pissed at myself for misjudging him. Mistakes like that can be fatal. I realize that the problem is I'm distracted by Davis. My anger for him is affecting me, now that I know I might have a shot at taking him down. And by taking him down, I mean killing him in an ungodly horrible fashion you don't want to read about. Well, okay. No. Not really. Probably. Look, I'm keeping my options open. No matter what, he has to be put away, and if he breaks a few bones on the way to Ops prison, well, that shit happens.

Once I'm home, I shower, check the computer to make sure Woody is still in the storage locker, then a text comes through with a call for 7:30. Great. I take it. I have to keep busy before my night surveillance on Davis.

Fortunately, the 7:30 goes well. He's a professional, some fat guy from San Francisco having a divorce party with his friends, who pay for my tip. It's straight sex, he's funny and happy, and I clear $2,700. This helps a little. I've made him happy and made decent, if not great, cash. Then I'm off for the night. I'm on duty to 11, but I know finishing with him at 8:40 doesn't really leave me much turnaround time.

I go home, kill time by looking at videos of bad drivers and then work as the Cube checking for leads online. Yeah, the Cube is more, like, say, Barbara Gordon as Oracle than Barbara Gordon as Batgirl. At least, this is what Olivia once told me. She dated some nerdy guy for six months who stuffed her head full of comic book information. Poor Olivia.

Men care about the stupidest things.

Chapter Six
Shelby and Olivia Back in the Day

"I miss you," I said when Olivia called at one in the morning. Her second show ended at eleven, but she went out to eat with the crew and showered before calling me from her hotel room.

"I miss you, too," said Olivia. "But I had a great show!"

"Good! I'm happy for you," I said, sounding like a turd in the toilet.

"You sound sad. What's wrong?" she asked.

"I just . . . it was a very agitating day."

"I can talk. I mean, it's Tahoe. Even the fucking bars are closed now."

I laughed. "No way."

"Okay, I'm exaggerating. Talk."

"Okay . . . I mean . . . I don't know why I let this bother me, but I ate cum off some guy's shoes tonight and it pissed me off."

"Really? That bugged you?"

I was surprised she was surprised. "Well . . . yeah."

"Haven't you done that before?"

"Well . . . yeah."

"It never pissed you off before. What's really got you pissed off?"

Then I realized where she was going . . . and that she was right. "I . . . staked out the warehouse. Davis. He was *there*, and I felt sooooooooooo angry." I took a breath. "I almost attacked him."

"I'm glad you didn't."

"What if he gets away?"

"He won't. That place is his business . . . and honey, I'm sorry about the cum eating thing, but I think we both know what you're *really* upset about."

"Yeah . . . sure, yeah, I've done worse."

"We both have. Life in entertainment."

I paused, then said, "Yeah, I guess. I'm just having a downer. I'll be fine tomorrow."

"Text me in the morning," she said. "Love you."

"Love you, too."

So . . . we're friend with benefits. We're more than that. But I guess, if I'm gonna be honest, and I always said I would after my mom's shit . . . we're friends in pain.

Olivia and I are both from Fullerton, which is this suburb of LA that's, you know, a typical suburb. It's stuck between Anaheim and Brea on the south and north and the 5 on the west and Placentia on the east. Has about 135,000 people, but you know, all of LA is just one big city at the end of the day. One of those typical California cities that was mostly white forty years ago and now is about split between whites and Hispanics. It has Cal State Fullerton and a St. Jude's hospital. And parks.

If you're not fucking math challenged, you can figure that I was born in 1998. I was eleven when my dad left us to have an affair with his secretary in '09. He later strangled her a year later and finally got convicted and went to prison in '16, so maybe it's not all so bad he left. He comes from a long line of assholes, of which the less said the better.

My mom was a beautiful woman, Sally Romaninsi. She had long, blonde hair, was like me. She grew up being molested by her perpetually drunk dad, went to college for one semester, and wound up a stripper. That's where she met dad. I'd imagine I was conceived in the back of a pickup truck.

Once dad was gone, mom . . . well, she had let herself go a bit, but she got back into shape real fast. She had been working as a dance instructor at a local fitness club. That wasn't going to pay the rent.

We had this nice home that had blue siding and white trim, a two-car garage, and a corner lot not far from school. Perfect home. But it had a price. Dad never paid shit for alimony even before he got tossed in the slammer. I figured this out pretty quickly as, after he left, slowly there were no new clothes, no steak on Sunday, no trips to the mall, the car window broke and wasn't fixed . . . we were slowly going broke.

That's when mom started having boyfriends. She moved around a lot. Jack, Sammy, Cesar, Cliff . . . after that, I started forgetting their names. Some touched me in, you can guess, the wrong places. I wouldn't put up with that shit. I told my mom, and she didn't put up with that shit either. But even the nice ones didn't last long. No one wanted to inherit my dad's debt . . . namely, me.

I came home from eighth grade one day and caught my mom by surprise. Guess she lost track of the time. I entered via the garage, then walked from the garage across a porch to the main house. Usually, I'm noisy, but in this case the main door was open as it was hot and, of course, the a/c was broken. So, I just opened the screen and stopped for a bottled water and heard a moan.

Look, I was thirteen and had internet access. I knew what that moan was about. Curious, I snuck through the messy house with shit everywhere and dodged the three sleeping cats and sleeping dog. Mom's bedroom was in the back.

The door wasn't shut. I peeked inside and found her on all fours on the bed taking it up the backside. Whoa. This was a little gross for me, as it would be for any thirteen-year-old, but that wasn't what upset me. No, I was upset by seeing five, one-hundred-dollar bills on the nightstand that hadn't been there when I went to school.

The guy giving it to her was someone who looked like a fat plumber who was named Al. I think.

Most girls would have slunk back to their room, but I was shocked by the money. I was wearing year-old jeans and riding in a car with barely any brakes and two broken windows while I ate candy bars for lunch because they were cheap. And she had this cash on the nightstand.

Moving into the doorway, I threw up my hands over my mouth and did my best acting job. "Oh, God, *Mother*!"

"Shelby!" she shouted, turning around with this God-awful look of horror on her face. Imagine if you had your period in the middle of a school assembly while speaking on stage, and that's how she looked.

Al pulled out and got soft really fast, grabbing his pants and nearly tripping himself as he got dressed. Mother grabbed this ancient pink robe she had hung on the doorknob and hustled me into the bathroom, where she shut and locked the door.

"Shelby, oh, I'm sorry, honey!"

I looked at her. "It's just sex, Mom. But what's the cash about?"

"He's just helping out."

I gave her a look of utter disbelief, like when a teenager tells her parents the drugs she's got in her backpack are for her friends.

"Really," she said empathetically, clearly sensing my skepticism.

"Sure, Mom, *sure*," I said, not being sarcastic, but clearly not sounding convinced either.

"Honey, baby, this house doesn't pay for itself. Do you know how *expensive* things are?"

I looked at her. "Mom . . . you always told me to be true and honest. You told me you were more upset at Dad that he lied about the affair than the actual affair. So, you had better take your own advice."

She looked really shocked, as if I'd pissed in her bed like a dog or something. "What?"

"Mom, you're just whoring yourself out!"

She slapped me.

Now, in retrospect, I could have, shall we say, chosen my words better. I mean, the "whoring" phrase was bound to produce, as Olivia would say, a negative reaction due to its negative connotation. I could've just said, "Mom, you fuck men for money like a prostitute, but I'm okay with it." But I was pissed off that she was lying to herself the same way Dad lied to us and the same way she told me never to act.

I merely stepped back and said, "Feel better?"

Her face cracked and she started to cry. Then she ran away and locked herself in her bedroom.

So much for family conversation.

I went to my room. When dad had been there, we would actually occasionally go to church. That hadn't happened in a while. I wasn't really a Christian, but I did believe in God and in prayer. But most of all, I believed in being true and honest to oneself. God made us to be ourselves. So be yourself. If you're a serial killer who eats people, don't blame society. Look in the mirror and man up before you pull out the bar-b-que sauce.

We are what we make of ourselves.

And I was going to stay true to that.

Now, things changed a bit a few weeks later. By now, she had moved on to a guy named Mike Zack. He was a guy with blond hair and a barrel chest, blue eyes, great body. Why he wanted my mother was a mystery to me, except maybe she was cheaper than the average hooker, but a guy like this could get any woman he wanted.

I was kind of naive about men at the time. Remember, I was thirteen.

Anyhow, he was an artist, did something called storyboards for movies. So, he worked at home, so he was able to come over a lot. My mom looked like a hamburger patty after about two weeks. But I did notice the broken screen door got fixed, the car window got fixed, and we started keeping the air conditioning on at night.

Anyhow, one Saturday afternoon, he came over while I was sitting in the living room watching TV. I was wearing blue shorts and a white camisole, you know, casual stuff. I remember I was watching this movie from the 90s called *Flatliners*. It was kind of creepy.

Real life was about to get creepier.

As I've told Olivia, I don't completely remember how it started . . . I was into the movie and Mike came in. Mom was still at the grocery store. I got up and let him in, we had brief small talk. He went into the kitchen.

The next thing I knew, someone grabbed me off the couch and threw me on the floor and began pulling down my shorts. I tried to scream, but a hand was over my mouth.

He moved fast and he was a big and built motherfucker. I had no chance of getting free.

Well, no chance if I were normal . . . which I was about to discover I wasn't.

I focused hard and tried to shove him off. The next thing I knew, the fucking floor was flipping us up in the air and I heard a shriek from wind and glass breaking. He flipped off me and crashed into the ceiling, then fell back down. I rolled out of the way to avoid being crushed and he hit the floor face first. He was out colder than a well-digger's ass, as Dad used to say.

I stared at him, then realized the living room was fucking trashed.

"What did I do?" I asked myself.

I checked, and he was out but breathing. I started to panic. What do I do now?

That's when my mom came in.

"*Shelby*!" she shouted, racing to me, dropping the two bags of groceries she had been carrying. So much for the eggs and bananas.

"Mom!" I raced to her and threw myself into her arms and began crying.

"Baby! *Baby*!" she said, holding me tight. She was crying, too. She knew something terrible had happened.

"He tried to rape me!" I finally gasped.

She pulled out her phone, but I knocked it away.

"No, mom, no! I'm not going through that! No! Just tell him to go away! *Make him go away*!"

For the first time in my life, my mother had a look of resolve. She nodded to me and said, "Go to your room and lock the door. Take my phone. If anything goes wrong, call 9-1-1."

"Mom, please, I'm scared!"

"I'll *handle* it," she said.

She pushed me gently, so I raced to my room and locked the door. I felt light-headed and dizzy. I still didn't know I had channeled. That realization would come much later.

I listened at the door.

I heard her moving. Finally, I heard water splashing and heard him wake up.

Then I heard a gun cock. I knew Mom had a .22. She'd bought it after dad left us and there were a couple break-ins at homes across the street.

She said sounding like a fucking female Clint Eastwood, I swear to God, "I know what you did. You get the fuck out of my house and never come back. If I or my daughter ever see you again, you're dead."

"I read you," Mike said evenly.

Then I heard footsteps, the door slam, and a car start.

I unlocked the door and came out to find my mom in the hallway, shaking and white as the paper you're reading this on. She was so soaked in sweat it looked like she'd finished a forty-minute cardio workout.

"I . . . he's gone," she said.

I just hugged her. I didn't know what to say. I had never known how strong my mom was until that moment.

No matter what terrible day you have — be it raped, beaten up, kid dies, car crash, a lawnmower chops off your pecker — there is always the day after. And that day after is a major bummer, because the fatigue after that stress is like . . . let's put it this way. I'd rather take on sixteen guys in an all-night orgy than wake up the day after the living room blew up again.

Mom never asked how the living room got fucked up. I guess it didn't matter, or she went into denial, or just figured Mike fucked it up trying to rape me.

Form that day on, our relationship was much stronger. We spent more time together. We binged on Netflix for several days as I recovered . . . and she did as well. I assured her many times he never got inside me, which he didn't. Still, it was pretty traumatic.

I learned my mom was a tougher person that I thought. And I learned how much she loved me.

However, I still had to learn how I had thrown that fuck-face onto the ceiling in the first place. That required research on the web, or so I thought.

A week after I was nearly raped, I was called to the guidance counselor's office. This was never a good thing. I wasn't planning for college, follow? However, I didn't do drugs and I hadn't been caught fucking anyone and wasn't pregnant, so I wasn't sure what this was about. My grades sure weren't winning awards, either, but they weren't bad enough to warrant a call to the guidance office. I mean, not without calling half the school there as well.

I was wearing a black hoodie, jeans, and a fake nose ring. I walked *reallllllllllly* slow to the office. The guidance counselor was this big fat man named Pat who had a mean bitch of a wife. He was bald and fat but nice. We all liked him. We hated her.

But on reaching his office, I saw someone else there. I sized him up quickly — forty-five years old, his brown, curly hair had now mostly faded to gray. He was slightly balding but looked distinguished rather than old. A short man, I'd go with five-eight, kind of wiry and I bet he still worked out daily, probably by jogging based on the frame.

He wore blue dress pants and a mint green dress shirt with a white tie. Initially, you think insurance agent, but then you could see his eyes and the intensity, and then it's more like supervisor or manager of some financial unit.

"Uh, hi," I said shyly as I knocked on the side of the open door.

"Come in, Shelby. This is Mister Sam Grant from the government."

My eyes widened, and I felt hot and clammy. Nervously, I shook his hand and said, "Uh, hi."

"Hi, Shelby, it' snice to meet you. Pat, could we have some privacy?"

"Of course. I'm more than happy to take a long lunch," he said, patting his fat belly which had busted a button on his white dress shirt.

Once he left, Sam shut the door and said, 'Don't be nervous, Shelby. Here's my card."

He hands me this card that is super-sleek. It's fucking embossed. All it says is this:

SAM GRANT, DIRECTOR OF FIELD OPS

"What's a field op?" asked, nervously sitting down in Pat's chair, which was huge and warm from his fat ass sitting in it all morning.

"It's part of Special Operations. We handle the paranormal for the government."

My face obviously showed alarm. "That has nothing to do with me."

He smiled politely. "It's okay, Shelby. We have a field office in downtown LA. You must have used channeling a week or so ago. We got a hit on it. If we weren't busy stopping paranormal criminals and natural disasters, I'd have been over here sooner."

"Why?" I asked defensively. "Are you here to arrest me?"

He laughed. "No, dear, no. I'm here because you're a channeler."

Again that word. "What does that mean?"

"Paranormals are rare, Shelby. There's only maybe a hundred in the whole world." He paused. "Most are elemental channelers. They channel the ancient Greek elements of earth, air, wind, and fire."

"Uh, huh. Is that what you do?"

'No, I have no abilities. I mostly sit around and push paper and tell people what to do," he said with a smile.

He seemed nice. But I didn't trust him. Yet. "Why are you here? I haven't channeled. I'm nobody."

"You don't have to be," he said.

I looked at him. "Why are you here?"

"Because you're in junior high school, which can be hard for the paranormal. Our office can help you learn about your abilities safely, and more importantly, give you protection."

"From what?" I asked, alarmed.

"Anything. Has someone attacked you?" he asked.

"No, why? *No,*" I lied, and not very well. Trust me, as a hooker, I've gotten *soooooooooo* much better at lying. Baby, size doesn't matter. See?

"I see. If you ever want to talk, I work with some nice women."

"Sure. So this channeling, it's normal?"

"Rare. But natural."

"Oh. Well, too bad, I can't do it."

He looked at me. I was sure he knew I was lying. But instead, he rose and said, "Keep the card. You can call anytime if you need help for anything. No strings, Shelby."

I put it in my purse "Sure. Can I go back to class? Miss Mortmeyer hates me, and this will make her hate me more."

He smiled. I shook his hand.

And I raced outta there, about to wet my pants. He scared me. I wasn't leaving my mom. I wasn't letting anyone find out what Mike tried to do to me. So, I wasn't letting anyone find out what I could do.

But now I did know for a fact . . . I could do *something*.

Not that it helped much immediately. I spent the summer working at a furniture store and then started high school. High school is Hell, as you all know. Anyhow, as pretty as I am now, and now I am one fine piece of ass, I wasn't all that pretty in school. I didn't care to be. I was known as kind of a wicca girl, you know, the weird type that does drugs and is a loner and keep to themselves. I wore a nose ring, fake, but still. That was enough to keep most people away. I didn't actually do drugs, but that was my rep.

A few kids were interested in me because I was different. But for the most part, everyone gave me a wide birth, because I was known as having a temper. One guy tried to touch my ass once. I slapped him and kicked him in the balls. Once that story got around school, I got a wide birth. For most teens, that would be a fate worse than death, but I was *glad* for it.

But no matter what you do, you can't push away everyone, damn it. Near the end of my freshman year, I was fucking around on the quad picking my nose or something and was approached by Olivia. She was this skinny ass girl with brown hair that was a fucking mess, wearing this starry sky, printed blouse and jeans that basically advertised she had no fucking hips. She looked pretty, although she had an inverted cross earing set.

"Hey," she said.

"Hey," I said.

We were sizing each other up. I was sitting in the grass, and she was standing, so she had the power dynamics in her favor. It was a nice day, and I was actually in a good mood. For a change.

"I'm Olivia," she said.

"Shelby. What's up?"

"Are you really into magic and stuff?"

I studied her. She was aggressive — no, assertive — but I sensed she was scared, too. I sure was. But I liked her. I knew her on campus, of course. She had her own core of friends and was one of those people that seemed to get along with everyone.

"Yes. I mean, I like weird stuff," I said, not sure where this was going.

"You ever do weird stuff?" she asked, and the way she said it . . . boy, that went right through all my defenses.

"I threw a guy through the ceiling once."

Her eyes lit up. "Damn! Look, I want to be a magician. A *real* one, not just puling rabbits out of hats. I could do that when I was seven. You want to help me?"

I shrugged. I knew this was about more than rabbits and magic. "Sure. I have time."

Two days later, we were at the school's theatre. This was a Friday. We were in jeans and hoodies, 'cause it was kind of chilly for April, and standing by a table with magic props on it. She had just shown me her act.

"It's good," I said sincerely.

She studied me. "I know. But I'm convinced — convinced, Shelby — that there's *real* magic in the world. Only it's not just magic. It's some sort of . . . ability."

Our eyes met and I frowned. I wasn't sure where this was going, but I was nervous. "I see . . . what is it then?"

"I don't know. But it's there."

It was like she was looking through me, like she could read my mind. She was hypnotic. Or I was an easy mark. I just . . . I had to tell her. I had to tell someone!

"It . . . I can do things, Olivia. That ceiling story wasn't bullshit. Watch."

I blew her props onto the floor.

She turned and smiled. "Oh, that's good. That's good!"

"What do you do?" I asked.

She turned sad. "Long story. It's different." She looked around and started picking up her props. "It's not private here. Let's go to my house and talk. Mom is over at Grandma's."

Olivia's house was a couple miles away, not far from my house, really, close to Hillcrest Park. Place was fairly nice but laid out really weird. It had a white stucco, tile roof, a big-ass garage, sitting on a corner under two big trees. The property was as small as a midget's dick. I mean, you could mow the yard in five minutes. Anyhow, it was long and rectangular.

Inside, the kitchen was cute but dated, strictly 1999 with big orange cabinets that were scratched up by cats, white backsplash, white counters, black stove. You know, typical stuff. The fridge was covered in magnets and a white board which had a lot of old notes clearly long ignored. The counters were covered in bowls of food, pencils and pens, keys, recycling bags, and just about anything else you can throw on a kitchen counter.

They had three cats: Maple, Chestnut, and Hickory. You can figure it out. They were all black, all long hair, all vomiting all the time. But they were cute. The house had two bedrooms, both tiny, a living room, and a kitchen. Seriously, the garage was almost as big. And there was a pool in back. Her dad used to have a workshop in the garage, but now it was empty and full of leftover pool furniture.

They no longer used the pool. You'll understand why soon.

She opened the fridge. I asked for a beer. She handed me a water and said, "You'll drink this. Beer rots your brain."

"Okay," I said, a little dumbfounded.

We sat on this beat up couch covered in about fifty blankets because the long-haired black cats left hair everywhere. Her house was old, like someone decorated it in 1999 and never upgraded. And sterile. No pictures. Just lots of cat hair hanging from . . . everywhere.

Olivia looked at me. "You're an elemental channeler."

I was stunned. I'm sure it showed. This was what that Sam guy had said. "How . . . what do you mean?"

She looked at me with a sly, confidential look and sipped her water. "My dad had . . . he could do things. It's why I got into magic. He wasn't an elemental channeler. But that's what you are. You have to be careful. If the wrong people find out, they'll try to use you, try to hurt you."

I was stunned. "I just . . . I don't know what I can do."

"I don't either. We can find out. But don't tell anyone. Maybe if you are bored and watch my magic act, I can help you learn your powers."

I laughed. "I *like* your act!"

She smiled. "Thanks. One other thing . . . you *must* learn to get along with people. The sullen teen thing won't hold up. If you're going to make it in this world, you gotta believe in yourself and you have to get along with others."

I made a face. "Why?"

"Because life is a team sport," she said.

"I don't know . . . I don't like sports."

She put a hand on my shoulder, "Then think of it as learning about who you can trust and who you can't. Because . . . look, I know something happened to you. Channelers manifest during stress."

I looked scared. She was gentle and said, "I'm here to listen if you want to talk. Or we can go get tacos. It's up to you."

Having someone to talk to . . . I felt so unburdened. I had felt so alone . . . and scared. "My . . . my mom . . . this is embarrassing."

"I have secrets, too. I'll share, though not today."

"She fucks for money, okay. She's a housewife hooker. One of the guys," and my voice was soft, "He tried to rape me."

"Damn."

"He didn't. I blasted him into the ceiling. Then mom pulled a gun on him and sent him away."

"Baby, I'm sorry. That is shit."

"That's . . . my suck-ass life."

"Your dad out of the picture?"

I nodded. "Banged the secretary when I was a kid, moved away with her, we never heard from him again until he got arrested for killing her. He's in some big prison up north somewhere."

She nodded and looked sad, but then she said, "I'll help you. You're my friend. Deal?"

"Deal."

"I'm not hiding things," she said cautiously. "I have to work up the courage to tell you about myself."

"It's your choice, baby," I said. "I'd like to know."

"You will."

I was curious why she didn't tell me about herself. I later realized she was just too fucking scared to tell me about her father.

A couple weeks went by. Then there's this Friday night. We went to see a movie, some sort of earthquake disaster movie that was pretty lame. We went back to her house. Her mom was at her grandmother's over in Huntington Beach, so we had the place to herself.

She found some leftover donuts in the fridge and offered me one.

"Uh, no way. Got any booze?"

"We can't sneak it here. I don't want to piss Mom off, and it rots your brain anyhow. Besides, I want to talk about something," she said.

I was surprised by how serious she appeared. That scared me, but also warmed me, because I knew she was about to trust me with something important. "Okay, sure."

"Let's go to my bedroom."

We went there. She fed the fish and was quiet. I sat on the bed, which she had made that morning, and enjoyed the smell of fresh sheets. Her room was dark and full of candles and lace curtains and a weird orange and black bedspread. There was makeup and magic shit piled everywhere: on the desk, the dresser, the floor, and even hanging from the curtain rods.

The lights were dim, and it was dark out. I asked her, "Uh, can we have some lights."

Suddenly, she turned and looked at me with a sad face. "I haven't told you the truth about my dad."

I tensed up, but said calmly, "Well, what's the truth? He Ted Bundy's cousin or something?"

She stood before the fish tank, which was well lit, so that put her in something of shadow. She clasped her hands together, put them to her mouth, and then said so softly I had to strain to hear, "We're friends, Shelby. I trust you with everything. And we have skills. But . . . I've done things that . . . my father raped me."

I cocked my head. "That's terrible!"

She slowly approached and sat on my right and said, "Don't look at me. I'm only telling you this because I owe you the truth. And if you hate me for this or don't want to be friends, that's okay, I understand, but we can't go any farther as friends or paranormal buddies or whatever we are without my being honest. I know you've been honest with me."

"I have," I said.

"Because you always are. You are without pretense and sometimes brutally honest." She paused. "Good traits."

"I think so."

"Father . . . here's what happened. We were out by the pool," she said, nodding at the window where the curtains were drawn. "It was afternoon, my mom was at my grandmother's, and he was drunk." She paused. "He had made me blow him, Shelby, many times before."

"I'm sorry," I said with pity.

"Don't . . . don't talk. Just listen."

"Sorry."

She was staring at the fish, which was staring back. "He approached me, and I knew I couldn't avoid it. He was a big man. I was lying back on a chair in a bikini. I . . . I couldn't stop him without a fight. I was terrified. But I had my phone, keys, and the security camera remote next to me. I'd been waiting for this chance. He always turned the camera off before, you know. I turned it on." She took a deep breath. "He was on me. I begged him to stop. I told him to stop. I finally stopped fighting and . . . he entered. God, it hurt. I've heard about women being raped and going numb. I wish that had happened to me, because it felt like being ripped in half by a wolverine.

"And . . . so it ended fast. Not even a minute. He got out, said thanks, and said if I said anything he'd kill grandmother."

She was shaking now and perspiring, as if in a street fight. I put a hand on her right thigh, but she didn't notice, or if she did, she didn't respond.

"I grabbed the phone and in fury waved it at him like a gun. I shouted and told him it was all on a live line to Mother."

She paused, and I almost thought she had passed out. Finally, she said, "He turned pale, then red, then came after me. But he didn't make more than five steps before he grabbed his chest and cried out in pain.

"I knew it wasn't a trick. I knew the security camera was backed up, so it didn't matter if it was a trick to get the remote or my phone, but it wasn't. He fell backwards and hit his head on the concrete.

"He wasn't breathing. I screamed in terror. I hadn't meant to kill him or hurt him even. I just wanted to make sure he couldn't hurt me or anyone else again. I was just going to tell him to go away and never come back.

"He was wide eyed but dead, his tongue out. The picture of death is horrible . . . horrible. I've seen it many times since, and you do get used to it, but the first time . . . it's grotesque."

"I'm sorry," I said, forgetting to be silent for a moment.

"I know you are," she said. "Anyhow, Uh, I didn't want him to die. I didn't know what was wrong with him, but I wanted him alive. I didn't want him to die because I'm not mean, and besides, I didn't want to be a killer.

"So, I desperately tried CPR, although I'm sure the head blow killed him as much as the heart attack. I tried so hard . . . and then things . . . got really weird."

She paused a long time again.

"I saw colors and . . . auras. I saw his soul, floating. Others, watching. And I saw his body begin to move, but the eyes were still dead. He started to rise, but he was dead, a zombie. I screamed like a little girl seeing a snake. I mean . . . it was blinding terror.

"The fear made my concentration drop. I didn't fully convert him to zombie. I just animated the corpse, which got up and once on its feet, fell down again. That cracked the skull and his brains leaked out.

"It was not pretty," she said shaking her head over and over and over.

"Then what?" I finally asked, not sure she was finished.

"I called 9-1-1. The police came . . . I don't remember all of it. They saw the video. The video also picked up his heart attack. Mom . . . she supported me . . . but she was hurt badly. That's when she really got into those downer pills."

"Yeah, well, I can imagine," I said.

"Yeah." She paused, still refusing to look at me. "That . . . that is what I had to tell you. Because if we're going to be friends, or whatever, you had to know. And if you think I'm a bad person because of this, then that's okay, too. You can leave. And if you ever tell anyone this, I'll deny it . . . and I'll hurt you."

I sat, realizing she had put forth the challenge flag.

I knew all she really needed was validation.

I paused a moment, then said, "It was an accident. He was your father, but he was a bad person. I don't blame you for anything."

Suddenly, she looked at me with huge, wet eyes. The relief on her face was stunning, shocking, and wonderful.

She grabbed my face, a palm on each cheek and pulled my face towards her and kissed me.

I had kissed boys, of course, and Evelyn Molitor in gym class when we both just wondered what it felt like.

Nothing ever felt like this kiss — not before or since.

Truly, it was awesome.

She pushed me to the bed and was all over me, moaning, kissing my cheek, ears, and neck. I moaned, getting wet. I couldn't believe what was happening, but I didn't care. The intensity of her need, her passion, her . . . well, just her . . . was overwhelming.

After kissing me for three, four minutes, she paused and said, "Thank you. I love you, Shelby. I love you so much for being there for me. You're all I have in the world."

Instantly, I responded. "I feel the same. I always will."

Then I pulled her back to me to kiss her passionately.

We then moved without talking, overwhelmed by passion and fear and excitement and a thousand feelings all at once. We got off the bed and stripped. Then I kissed her, and we rubbed each other's butts while we were kissing. She was so wet she was leaking down her legs.

I looked into her eyes as I broke the kiss and said, "I want to taste you."

She just nodded. I think she was too excited to speak.

She sat on the edge of the bed, and I knelt between her legs. I will tell you honestly, I had no fucking clue how to give head at that point. I was carried by enthusiasm, not technique.

That was more than enough. She suddenly clamped her legs together and screamed like she was being murdered as she had an orgasm. Lemme tell you, after that, I was eager to find out what the fun was about. Provided I lived. She almost suffocated me!

Then we switched. Like me, she was all enthusiasm and no skill, but shit, when you're that age, what do you care?

I felt it coming, a deep, powerful orgasm. I'd had sex before, but never had an orgasm. Little boys just can't hold it. Anyhow . . . it was awesome. Like fucking totally awesome.

Then we were exhausted. She got up and lay next to me and we held each other and just enjoyed ourselves.

After a while, I turned and asked her, "Why did you tell me tonight?"

"I had to. I couldn't stand waiting anymore, to know if I would be accepted or rejected."

"I will never reject you. Never," I said seriously.

She nodded. "I know that now."

I kissed her with kindness, then asked, "What . . . what do we do now?"

"We'll figure it out. No telling anyone. My mom will shit herself, and I don't want to be known in school as the weird lesbian witch couple."

"Ah, those fuck-faces probably think that already," I said.

She laughed. "You're right. But we don't have to advertise."

"Are we . . . like a couple?" I asked.

She looked at me. "I don't know what we are. We're paranormal friends. I think that's like a whole new category of friend with benefits."

I laughed. "That's it. PFWB. That's us."

She smiled. "But you know I love you."

"And I love you."

We were intense for a moment, and then I cracked "We'll have to find husbands, though. We'll need someone to cook and clean for us."

She nearly died laughing.

That's how it started. Our relationship has gone through a lot over the years. We've had fights. We've had loves. We've each had and dumped boyfriends. We've each been though weird paranormal shit.

Her magic made her much more accepted in school than I was, which I didn't give a shit about. I was just marking time in high school to move on with life. I kept myself entertained finding boys I could fuck and actually getting into social classes like psychology and sociology and history that I could pass without any effort at all. Fuck math and science, that was me.

Olivia, she was better at school. She had her own little magic act and was in the drama club. Some of those guys were okay. We had a curly-haired guy who looked like Art Garfunkel named Zed, cool guy. He's in Hollywood now as a bit actor. And this chick named Rowanda.

Olivia and I learned about each other as much as we could, but we were mostly into kissing and spending time together. Sure, we got it on, but that wasn't always the goal. The goal was to enjoy each other.

And we were totem hunting. Totems helped Olivia's magic to no end. They helped me a little. I mean, they got me through math with a "C," which I did not earn.

We both decided early in senior year to move to Vegas. Olivia already had interest from the Magic House, and I had no reason to stay in fucking Fullerton. While I was in high school, mom had gotten a bit . . . out there. She had found out about prescription pills and spent much of her day zonked. Our relationship again deteriorated. In a way, it's kind of sad. But in a way, Mom was, I think, glad to have me gone. Now she could fuck for money as much as she wanted and pretend it was all perfectly normal. I tried to help her and understand her. But she never. . . fuck, she never grew up.

As for me . . . I was gonna fuck for money, too. I wasn't going to have people or a job run my life, and I wasn't going to be broke. Olivia did okay as an apprentice at the Magic House, but I had to make the serious cash. She has that Stinger because of me. And she had to deal with typical entertainment bullshit. She fucked the owner of the place, who was 48 and had to give up magic because he hurt his back. Harvey Fendleman. Douche.

I had no problems being a hooker. I like helping people, and I wasn't too worried about getting hurt, since I could channel. I was pretty good looking. And the cash . . . yeah, any doubts I had vanished the first two nights when I cleared seven grand.

Do I sound greedy?

Well, then you've never been poor, so fuck you.

Chapter Seven
The Origin of the Cube

Kickboxing was on the order Wednesday morning. I got up at 8:30, had plenty of coffee, fed the cat, and checked my email and social media. No breakfast, not before workout.

My appointment was at ten. I did some major ass kicking and coach was proud of me.

I got home about 11:15, took a long shower, and relaxed in my robe. I was on call 1-9, having asked to shift my hours up, because I wanted to make sure I had time as the Cube to stake out Davis' warehouse. Like I've said before, I'm one of the top girls at the agency, so Nina didn't have a problem with it.

As it turned out, it was a busy day. I had three sessions, and by nine I felt like a beef patty. It had been a busy week, definitely busier than normal, especially on top of that fucking trip to New Mexico to nab that serial killer asshole and dealing with Woody. I was checking on him, by the way, but he was enjoying reading in the storage locker. He'd been busy. I don't think he ever actually started Brad Thor, just went right to the classics. He'd made it through <u>War and Peace</u> and had moved on to <u>Moby Dick</u> and now was reading something called <u>The Odyssey</u>. I guess it's a spy book.

My first appointment was a regular, Tony Sanchez, this guy into stock trading. He works at home, has this huge fucking palace west of town that is only accessible by a guarded dirt road. He's worth a lot. I've bene fucking him for two years, and he usually tips ten grand. Imagine a really fat Robert Downey Junior and you've got him. Anyhow, we had fun. We did it three times. He was in a mood. Then we talked for about an hour. He's a professional, but he was chatty today. He made something like two million the last three days, so he was all wired. He talked about his family in Philadelphia and the weather and music. He's interesting. He also sent me home with some good wine and a box of cookies he had sitting around, a gift he couldn't eat because he's diabetic.

I got home, showered, got another call. This was a third-timer with me, Eddie Polaski, some type of military official down in California. He was on leave. We had a blast.

The last call was, however, a little different. I had gotten home and showered again. Believe me, I used a lot of skin lotion. All this showering in a dry climate like Vegas was murder on the skin. Anyhow, Nina called just as I got out of the shower and I'm standing naked and white on the tile.

"Hi, Shelby. I have a third, it's going to be a double."

Doubles in our parlance meant I was going with a partner. "Sure. Who?"

"Shauna Holmberg. The client is a second-timer. Shauna worked with them before. They are a couple that like to 'force' two women to have sex with each other. While you two are getting it on, the clients screw each other."

I shrugged. "Easy money. I worked with Shauna a few weeks ago, like twice in that one week. She's fine."

"I knew that. You're in?"

"Yeah. I've been porked twice today. I'd be quite happy to take a non-porking assignment."

Nina laughed. "You're splitting the tip, so it's not going to be a big cash-cow."

"Will I clear at least a grand?"

"Yes, easy."

"I'm in. I just got out of the shower."

"Start dressing like a schoolgirl then. I'll text you the details."

Great. Schoolgirl. A common costume, so that was one that was on hand. But I was bored with them, so I decided it was a good chance to visit the storage locker, get an outfit, and check on Woody in person.

***

"What's up, legs?" he asked when I entered.

"Gotta get dressed for success," I said. "You okay? Need more books?"

"Hey, I'm a marionette. I have no need for creature comforts, and I'm still reading Homer's <u>The Odyssey</u> in between watching Dr. Phil."

"That guy will rot your brains," I said, checking the clothes rack.

"I assume you mean Dr. Phil and not Homer. How's my boss?"

"She had a good show last night," I said.

"Good. I like her. Her act is a little theatrical, but if I had her legs, I'd do it that way, too."

I looked at him. I still didn't trust him. I had my outfit, a red pleated skirt and white sweater. "I'm set."

"Hey, I gotta ask one thing. How did you wind up being a fucking superheroine? There's like forty versions online. Which is true?"

I made a face.

Now, you've heard a lot about being a hooker and not much about being a superheroine. Well, that's mostly because I planned to be a hooker and never planned on being a superheroine. It just happened.

Olivia and I were really focused on our careers and our new life in Las Vegas the first year. When I started as a call girl, of course, I had to start at an agency and work up. Once you get into the industry and prove yourself, you can work up and meet girls at better agencies and they bring you in, you know, that stuff. I was lucky. I was at my first agency, which was a dump, for only three weeks before I met Candy Denise. Yeah, one of those people with two first names for a first and last name, which usually is a bad sign, but not in Candy's case. She got me into the Empire, which was a huge jump in class and pay.

I worked my ass off that first year. I was doing five nights and three calls, and when I was having my time of the month, I was doing pegging and BJs and other stuff.

Olivia worked like a dog as well at the Magic House. She had to audition to get in, then had to fend off challengers, and of course had to sleep with the owner. All of that worked out.

So, we'd been working girls for about a year before the Cube came into the picture. I'd bought Olivia her car, and we'd each bought our starter condos. Cash. Olivia was already doing shows in Vegas and Phoenix, but hadn't broken into Southern California or the Pacific Coast yet.

June of 2017 was about a year since we arrived. Olivia liked to have flashy jewelry, because anything that distracts the client works in the favor of the magician. We tended to cruise pawn shops, because Vegas was the land of the rich and the desperate. Down to their last dollar, idiots from farm country were more than willing to put up the family jewels to get that last roll . . . and usually then go home dead broke. Too bad. If you're stupid enough to gamble away your ownings, I have no pity on you.

So, let's see . . . we were at a pawn shop and found this beautiful gem. We didn't know what it was. Neither did the pawn store owner. He figured it was, like, a space rock that broke up. It was about the size of a thumbnail, shaped like an oval, color of butterscotch. Olivia loved it instantly. She put the gem in a necklace and wore it three days straight in her practice, as she was between shows that week.

She got sick. Headaches, fatigue, weakness, and just blahhhhhhhhh. She accidentally left the necklace at my condo and then *I* got sick. This struck us both as shit-ass weird.

We did some research and thought it was a totem. Totems are objects that let people with latent paranormal ability manifest low-level TK type powers, like maybe throw a frisbee by the mind. Bullshit stuff.

But some were really powerful, and some worked even for those without latent paranormal ability.

Olivia knew about totems. I didn't know jackshit about them. Olivia did some research but found nothing.

As I got sick, Olivia got better. We decided to put it in the storage locker after her practice one Thursday in June. We got better. A couple days later, I met her at the Magic House. She had the totem with her, just to test our theory, and sure enough she started to feel the same . . . blahhhhhhhhh.

We left the Magic House. She was wearing jeans and a black camisole while I was wearing white dress shorts and a blue and white vertically striped shirt with new sandals. As we approached her Stinger, this totally wasted looking white chick came out from behind the dumpster. She had short, black hair, green eyes, a chipped front tooth, and was very pale. Wearing a jeans jacket over a black T-shirt with a skull, jeans, and black booties, she looked like a fashion disaster from 1994.

Seeing us, she pulled a gun.

I acted instantly, sending an earth channel down and a wind channel up. The earth channel dislodged her, and the wind hit her and blew her into the dumpster, where she dropped the gun.

Olivia picked up the gun. Our attacker was sitting against the back wall. I jumped on her lap and shoved my forearm into her neck and pushed her head against the wall.

"What the fuck are you doing, bitch? I paid cash for that car!" I shouted.

I relaxed a bit so she could talk. She coughed, then said, "I want my gem!"

I glared. "You got a name besides cumbucket whore? That's my new name for you."

"Jasmine. Jazzy."

I nodded at Olivia, who had the gun aimed at her. "My friend is the real bad-ass. She's a necromancer. She can channel the dead, send their spirits after you, even kill you with a touch."

This was an exaggeration, but, you know, I was making a fucking point. Jasmine nodded and said, "But it's *mine.*"

Olivia said, "What is it?"

"A water channeling totem," she said. "You didn't know?"

"No. I got it because it was pretty," said Olivia.

Jasmine glared, and I snapped, "Water channeling how? It flush the toilet for you?"

She glared back at me. "It slowly pulls the water out of the holder. They slowly dehydrate."

I looked at Olivia and she looked at me, surprise obvious on both our faces. Then recognition.

"Then what?" I asked.

She stared. "Then nothing. Then you're dead, jizz-face."

"Who were you planning to kill?"

"Fuck off."

I slapped her. Hard. "I'm not playing games, cumbucket whore."

"My boyfriend cheated on my best friend. I was going to give him the totem to pretend to make up with him and let him rot. But my fucking rent was late and then I got fired and had to hock it." She spit towards Olivia. "Then you bought it 'cause it's pretty. Jesus fucking Christ."

I pulled her to her feet and turned her around. Olivia took the cue and pulled handcuffs from her black and red stage magician's bag in the passenger seat of the Stinger. She often used real cuffs. Trick cuffs tended to fail at very bad times. I'll explain later.

"What the fuck are you doing? You can't arrest me, bitch," said Jasmine. She wasn't really a people person, was she?

"Sure can. C'mon, Olivia, let's see how roomy the trunk is in the Stinger."

She fought, sure. But Olivia put a hand out and channeled what she called the spirits of souls, and Jasmine turned white and started shaking. I picked her up and carried her fireman style to the car and dumped her ass in the trunk.

"Great. Now we've kidnapped her. Now what?" asked Olivia.

"I call that Sam guy."

"Who?"

"Sam Grant, the dude who came to see me back in high school."

"He's still in charge?"

I shrugged. "If he's not, I'll find someone who is. But we need help. We gotta get this gem off the street and do something with her. We can't just send her home to kill her boyfriend."

"Of course not," said Olivia. "You carry around his card?"

I had only a wallet on me, but it was in there. I pulled it out and waved it under her nose. "Always be prepared, baby."

Olivia rolled her eyes. "Somehow, hooker of the year spouting phrases of the Girl Scouts just seems wrong."

I laughed and called Sam.

"Yeah, I need Mr. Sam Grant . . . I'm Shelby Burnbeck, met him like four years ago when I was in high school in Fullerton, but I'm in Vegas now and have a problem, a gem . . . uh, some rude broad tried to take it, but we have her, uh, sequestered? Uh, under control . . . the Magic House . . . oh, yeah, that's it . . . twenty minutes? Cool! Thanks!"

I turned to Olivia. "Twenty minutes."

"Nice service. This guy must know his shit."

"This . . . is not a niece piece of jewelry," said Sam as he held the gem up to the light. He'd arrived in seventeen minutes. He was wearing black jogging pants with red stripes, a purple T-shirt, and white sneakers. He looked a little older, but I recognized him straight off.

"The bimbo in our trunk said it dehydrates a person. Slowly. We each got sick with it," I said.

Olivia added, "With symptoms that would fit dehydration."

He looked at me and smiled. "Don't think I'm stalking you, but I ran a check when the call came in. Glad to see you've moved to town. You like the call girl life or want to join us?"

I wanted to vomit. "Uhhhhhhhhhhhh . . . I'm good. I don't get along with government stuff. I appreciate the offer."

"We pay well and have great benefits."

I laughed. "So does Mr. John. Trust me, you can't afford me."

He laughed. "Well, your life is your business, but I'm always here." He looked at Olivia. "Same for you."

"Thank you, I appreciate the offer."

He held up a finger. "And, ladies, I have more good news. This totem is illegal. Ops offers cash for bringing them in, and we have seen a bit of an uptick in the market lately. This little butterscotch rock is worth five grand."

Olivia's eyes widened. "Damn! I only paid *fifty bucks* for it!"

She turned and we did a high-five.

"Hey, before you get too excited, the people that play with these are dangerous."

I thumbed at the trunk. "*She* wasn't much trouble."

"She's a user not a mover. Most of the movers are into other stuff, like drugs and sex trafficking, anything to make a buck. They aren't usually paranormal, but latent paranormals can use the totems."

"I can take care of myself, gramps," I said.

He laughed. "I know that. In fact, if you get more of these," and he held up the gem, "I'll give you cash. And if you ever need back-up, just call."

"Deal," I said.

"You want a check or electronic deposit?" he asked, putting the gem in a small tin box.

"Check is fine. If it bounces, I'll find you!"

He laughed. "Three days processing time. Text me your mailing address. Keep me posted if you make more interesting finds and be safe. Nice to meet you, Olivia."

"Sure."

Once he left, Olivia looked at me and said, "Hmmmmm . . . seems like he just conned us into doing his work for him."

"For five grand, that doesn't bother me! It'll help keep people safe, too."

"Oh, I agree."

"I can probably get a line on some of this stuff. People tell me everything. They think hookers are like doctors or won't tell or some shit. Let's work on this." Honestly, I was excited. I like helping people who needed help.

"I'm good with that, but we can't use the Stinger as our paddy wagon!"

We both laughed at that.

This was the start of the Cube, but not immediately. It was a few weeks later. I had a meet at Chevron located off the 15 on a Friday night. It was Wednesday, August 9, 2017, and hotter than fuck. It was also windy. Fucking dirt blew everywhere and my hair was a mess.

The meet was for eleven at night, but it was still nearly ninety degrees. And I came to the meet ready to be double-crossed, because my source was this shifty-assed motherfucker named Ralph Sanchez. He was a male porn star. He apparently used his totem to keep his dick up for incredible lengths of time. Don't ask more questions, I don't want to get into it.

Ralph was a Hispanic man with a good build but not much lower leg development, a thin mustache, a bit of a sneer, and a haircut straight out of 1986.

I wanted to be ready for anything, so I spent a shit-ass amount of money — I'm talking like the five thousand bucks we got for the butterscotch gem — and got this mostly Kevlar suit that was all dark blue, sort of like the color of the football team the Chargers, like it used to be, back when they played in San Diego. We'd get them on TV sometimes in LA. Anyhow, it covered me up to my neck. It would stop most things. Then I had a matching mask which covered most of my upper face. I looked like a really sexy cosplay gal, you know, one that knows what the fuck she's doing.

Ralph was parked in a '06 Mustang that was black with flame racing stripes at a stall near a public phone. Really, Vegas still had some. Anyhow, he was sitting in the driver's seat. I slipped into the passenger seat.

"Fifty?" I asked.

"For this, try three hundred. If you want to blow me, I'll give you fifty," said Ralph.

I gave him the finger and handed over three, one-hundred-dollar bills. "This better be good."

"It is." He gave me everything I wanted, then handed me a purple gem about the size of the tip of a pencil eraser. "That's it?"

"That's it."

"Thanks. Nice doing business with you."

He started the car. "Same. I'll keep my eyes open. I can always use a three-bill."

I got out and he left. I put the gem in a pocket in my suit, a carrier on the hip. Then I went to the Chevron's snack shop to grab a Pepsi and a Hershey's bar.

I walked into a robbery.

Really, I was kind of out of it, mulling over the info Ralph had given me and how such a tiny gem could do so much damage, and frankly a bit annoyed I had taken so many precautions and now was baking in this fucking Kevlar suit. More on that in a moment. But anyhow, I walk in and two white guys who look sort of like those Bo and Luke Duke guys on *Dukes of Hazzard* have shotguns and are taking the place down. Six people are on the floor.

"I put up my hands and said, "Whoa."

But as I did that, I channeled wind. Channeling isn't a super-power. It's kind of like being an artist. You make sense of the world around you and control the flow. Sorry, it just works that way. If you want normal super-powers, read a comic book or watch a Marvel movie. Anyhow, when you're indoors, wind is the easiest way to create a stealth attack. Earth channeling disrupts the ground, but then you gotta follow up with something. But wind is invisible and takes your target by surprise.

So, as I rose my hands, I channeled wind from behind me, because the door stayed open for a moment and, bam-o! Wind blew in and blew the two dumb motherfuckers into the freezers holding the milk and ice. They hit like water balloons off a frat building roof, splat!

One dropped his gun and was half stuck in the freezer. The other sort of got to his knees and still had his gun.

This is where those kickboxing lessons come in. I kicked that fuck-face under the chin. He yelped and went down cold. I picked the gun up, unloaded it, and threw it to the stunned clerk. The clerk was some Indian looking guy with a name tag Vishal. He was cute, wore glasses, had a nice build.

"That was awesome," he said with only a slight hint of an accent.

"Thanks.

Suddenly, one of the customers has a phone in my face. She had these giant, round blue eyes, black hair straight and parted in the middle, and a friendly face — and she was wound the fuck up.

"Hey, hey, you're a superhero! I've heard about you guys. Who are you? You have a tag? What are your powers?"

I looked at the phone and muttered, "I'm . . . uh. . . the Cube. Because I, uh, control earth, air, wind, and fire, four things like . . . uh, a Cube."

Yeah, right, *you* come up with something better on the spur of the moment in the middle of the night when someone shoves a phone camera at you, fuck-face. Anyhow, it wasn't my best moment, but it didn't matter.

"Damn! Thanks for saving us!"

"You're welcome. I don't have time for questions. Bye!" I shouted.

I raced outside, alarmed they might try to pin me in or find out who I was or offer me a Smoothie or some shit. I ran and got several blocks away to a secret tunnel that I knew led back to a parking lot I could use to get home the back way.

Of course, the next day my face was all over the internet and my, ah, interview was being shown everywhere. God, how embarrassing.

Just for the record, the dumb-fucks holding up the place got 26 months and are butt-buddies in some prison right now, so it was worth it.

Some of my other superheroine adventures . . . not so much. The worst was the one with the cat. You must've seen that one, right? Yeah, so this one night around one in the morning in July . . . I guess it's at least two years ago now . . . I'm on a meet with an informant in one of those low-level warehouses that lay along the access roads on the west of the 15. The guy's name was Wendell Hickman, who is doing a nice ten to twenty now for cocaine peddling. Anyhow, he had info on a totem scheme moving product to Oakland. God knows why anyone would move anything to Oakland other than a bomb to raze the place, but hey, everyone is different.

We meet at this warehouse, you know the type, wide and flat. Half of it was empty. We met on the roof, to make sure no one would overhear. I come up the fire escape, and there's Wendell. He's blond on blue, shaggy hair, shaggy beard, glasses, looks like an accountant on a bender. Wearing clothes way to big, black T-shirt and jeans. Nervous. Twitchy. Looking around constantly.

"I'm the Cube. Hickman?"

"Who else would I be?" he snapped.

"Sorry. Here," I said, handing over $100. He was a cheap buy.

He took the money and said, "The shipment to Oakland leaves from next door tomorrow. There's at least fifty totems. They're gonna kill everyone, all fourteen employees, and shut down the operation."

"So, you're talking because you're squeamish, huh?"

"Yep. I'm outta here. I got a flight to Seattle booked that leaves in two hours. Thanks for the cash."

"You're welcome. Don't spend it all in one place."

I hop down. He goes down the ladder on the other side, as agreed, and leaves in his silver BMW. I hang around, just making sure he was alone. I ponder his find, and immediately decide to call Ops and let them handle this. No way am I going into a potential firefight like this on my own, or even with Olivia.

I walk along the alley and make a call to them on my cell while I walk. Sam Grant had quit by this time, so I got someone named Little Jack McGrath. All I know about him is he had giant ears. Anyhow, I give her the info. Then I walk between this warehouse and the next, and this puts an abandoned corner of the warehouse to my right. Used to be a nudie bookstore, I think. Anyhow, I hear the unmistakable "meow" of a cat.

I look up. There's this pretty, tiny little tortoiseshell cat, a mix of mud brown and black with huge, scared eyes. It's on this wooden beam over what had been the door, and it's clearly terrified to jump.

It just keeps meowing at me. I look around, because the beam is about eight feet up, too high to reach.

"Stay calm, kitty," I say.

I consider blowing her down, but I decide against it. I might push too hard and send her flying, and besides, it will scare her.

I go back to the alley and check the dumpster, and I find two bins full of crap. I dump the crap and use the bins. I stack them on each other.

I reach up and say, "You're safe, kitty."

At this point, the stupid kitten jumps off and runs away, causing me to step back suddenly. This causes the bins to collapse, and I go flying, landing flat on my ass.

"Stupid cat," I mutter.

Then I dust off my ass and head home.

The next day, I wake up to this shit:

SUPERHEROINE DISSED BY CAT!

SUPERHEROINE HATES CATS!

SUPERHERO WANNABE FALLS FLAT ON ASS!

CAT 1, CUBE 0

Yes, these are just a few of the headlines that greeted me. I was picked up by a surveillance camera some workers digging a tunnel along the 15 had set up, worried their equipment might get stolen. Like anyone is going to steal a fucking earth-digger. Anyhow, some fine worker posted my adventure and made a total fool of me.

Boy, I was pissed.

Olivia thought it was cute. So did a lot of people. A lot of them hated me for calling the cat stupid. Well, he or she was. I never found out what happened to the cat.

Even worse, that aborted the entire totem moving plan. By three that afternoon, the warehouse had a mysterious fire that burned everything. Obviously, those in charge saw the publicity and realized I had been hanging around, and quickly moved to cover their tracks.

So, I not only didn't save the cat, I blew a chance for Ops to nail a totem move. Shit like this is why it's better to work alone. And shit like this is why social media is a tool of the devil. Although at least no one got hurt, and I accidentally saved fourteen people. All that really got seriously wounded was my ego.

The worst of it all was my ass hurt for three days.

Okay, that's the exception. I saved three people from being run over on the Strip last week. They were drunk and about to walk right into traffic when I tackled them. Although I was in my hooker guise then, so I guess for the Cube that doesn't count. I have gotten fifty-four people arrested and had a few pick suicide by cop, like that serial killer in New Mexico. And I've recovered eight totems. That's not bad.

I didn't tell all this to Woody. Fuck him. I didn't trust him. Instead, I completely ruined his thrill and said, "None of them. Have fun. Don't get wood rot. I'll check in on you tomorrow."

"Sure. No worries. I'm quite fine here."

I left. This whole fucking Woody thing was weird, even for me. I would be very glad when Olivia got back home, so we could deal with this and get things back to normal.

"Normal for them is to have us in, then start the role play. They use a fake gun," said Shauna, although her name as a hooker was Julie Corrigan.

We were outside the hotel room at the Luxor. I had worked with Shauna twice before. She was twenty-four with a two-year-old kid but looked hot. She had long, black hair straight with blue eyes and a good ass, normal breasts. She was quiet and thoughtful. About average height. She wore a blue and white pleated skirt and a blue sweater. We both had blue hairbands. I liked her, but she was not a big talker. I only knew about the kid because Nina had told me. But in our previous two encounters, we worked well together, though this would be the first time we'd be having sex with each other. We had met up in the elevator on the way up.

"Got ya."

"I'll take the lead. I know them," Shauna said.

"That's fine. I've been fucked already today. I'm quite happy to lie around and do as little as possible," I said, rolling my eyes.

She smiled. "You make a fetching schoolgirl."

"So do you. Ready?"

She nodded and knocked on the door.

A dude comes to the door, he's polite shows us in, and his wife is just inside. It's a suite, so the room is nice, has a nice view, but at the end of the day I know it's a hotel room with sheets washed by retarded guys.

No, really. Didn't I tell you this? Yeah, most hotels, the laundry is done on this federal work-for-hire program with the developmentally disabled. Even a retard can shove sheets in a washer, press a button, and take them out, then do the same with the dryer. It's a deal for the hotel. They pay them like two bucks an hour because it's one of those "good for society" deals, and this one actually is. I mean, no one with a brain is going to do that job. And no one is going to do it for two bucks an hour.

Anyhow, back to the couple, who were Tony and Michelle Rowe. I learned during our session that they're what the business world calls a power couple. They worked at the same place, this massive company that sells second-hand tech to places like Hollywood and other places who need disposable crap to blow up. And if they salvage something useful when a place goes under, they sell that, too. From what I learned, their big score was selling most of the equipment used in that first *Avengers* movie like a decade ago to be blown up by aliens.

There's money in this. They're worth seven figures.

Go figure.

The Rowes look like corporate types. In the 80s, they would've been called yuppies. He's tall, thin, and balding with his remaining black hair cut super short, a beard cut very short, and big ears. He's wearing a black suit. I figure him to be forty, but the background info says 46. And he's got the lean build of a runner.

She's old, too, forty-three and looks it, but not in a bad way. But she's got that cold, corporate look. She's got green eyes, kinky brown hair draped past her shoulder, and a thin frame. Average height, teeth, looks. A few freckles. She's wearing a dark blue blazer with white trim, matching skirt, and white hose. They look like they're about to conduct a board meeting.

Shauna as Julie takes the lead after the money is exchanged and said, "Shelby and I thought it best to interview for your positions."

I knew this was the trigger word to start the role play. Now, role play can be tricky. A girl I worked with once who now has three kids and lives in Portland, she gave me the best tip. Remember it's their fantasy, not ours. No matter how stupid or bizarre or even boring it might seem to you, to them it's ultra-hot sex night. She said it's like arguing with a person having hallucinations. You won't win. So, ride it out and go with it and hope it ends well. Role play is the same way.

Michelle folded her arms over her chest and says, "My position is demanding. Have you been with a girl before?"

"No, ma'am," said Shauna in this sultry whisper. Whoa. Now I see why her rep was that she got good tips. "I don't go that way."

Michelle glared. "Then why are you here?"

"I just . . . I need a job," said Julie softly.

"Then take your clothes off."

Julie did a great job of looking shocked. "Please, don't make me. Don't make me do this."

Michelle then pulled a gun from the back of her pants, pointed it at Julie, then snapped, "Shut up, slut! Get those clothes off!"

Then she swung the gun at me.

Now, I was no ordinary call girl. I was the Cube, superheroine of Vegas and feared by evildoers everywhere . . . with apologies to Day Man and those guys on that Philadelphia show. So, I was not the least bit intimidated. I mean, Julie had warned me, but I knew the gun wasn't loaded. The first thing I did when I decided to fight crime as the Cube was learn about guns. Second was learn about knives. That led to ordering all the Kevlar-type of shit.

Michelle smiled and said, "Strip, bitch."

I did as required, not out of fear, but out of the requirements of the job. I moved pretty fast. So did Julie. Once she was nude, I could see her body. She was a better looker than I remembered. She had really nice breasts and big nipples, like quarters, not pennies. She was also really tan.

Gesturing with the gun, she said to Shauna, "Julie, you slut, get on your knees and lick her pussy."

"But . . . I don't do those things," said Shauna shyly, obviously acting.

"You do now!" snapped Michelle.

Shauna nodded and actually managed to generate a fake tear. Then she dropped to her knees.

"Can I sit down?" I asked Michelle.

"You lay back on the bed, baby. The virgin here is going to eat you good, then you're going to get a meal of your own. You look like a slut. I bet you eat pussy every day."

"Sure, I love it," I said, moving to the bed and laying back. I spread my legs, and Shauna lay on her stomach in front of my privates.

"Ahhhhhhhh," I moaned as she made contact, and it was a real moan. I liked Shauna. She had sort of the look of Olivia, but she also knew what she was doing.

Men don't understand anything about eating pussy. It isn't just about the clitoris or about the vagina or about any of that. It's about patience. Girls take a while to reach that moment. Most men lick us like an ice cream cone and expect us to come in like two minutes like they do. It doesn't work that way.

Shauna was talented, and she was clearly enjoying it. Every once in a while, she put her head up and asked if she could stop, and of course Michelle said no.

After eight minutes, Shauna tapped my right hip hard three times. I figured she wanted me to fake it, so I moaned and slammed my legs together on her face and shouted, "Oh, I'm gonna come!" And then I faked my orgasm.

Michelle said, "Good job, you virgin slut. You. Slutty blonde. Get off the bed."

I did as she said, a little surprised. I'd figured from the play she was going to want me to eat her. Instead, she sat on the bed and put Shauna between her legs, gun pointed at her head.

I had Tony, as it turned out. He was sitting in a chair. He snapped his fingers and said, "Hey, I need attention, slut."

"Yes, sir," I said.

He came pretty quickly and had me rub it into my face. I'm okay with that shit. It washes off.

Then he told me, "Have a seat and watch the end of the show."

I was surprised. They made me watch. When they finished, Michelle came to me and said, "You slut. You got off watching it, didn't you?"

"Yes, ma'am."

"You want my pussy, don't you?"

"Yes, ma'am."

She turned and bent over. "You get this first. Clean it!"

I gave her a rim job. Hey, sucking ass isn't a problem if it's clean. It's kind of fun, in a dirty way. I ate her good, then he turned and shaved my face in her cotch. She came very quickly. Then she shoved me back onto the bed.

Then she went to her purse and took out a thousand-dollar bill as a bonus tip on top of an already good payday. She shoved it in my pussy and said, "You're a great lay." She did the same to Shauna. "Now get the fuck out of here so I can fuck my husband."

We got out, dressing fast. Once outside, I said to Shauna, "That was a profitable night."

"Yeah. I gotta go, though. I'm late and the babysitter has shit to do."

She quickly separated from me and got to the elevator, which was a little weird. Usually, girls talked a bit after those sessions, if nothing else just to be polite and come down from the high.

I was a little offended. Just a little.

But it didn't matter. Because I had been very well paid.

Once I get home, I take a long shower. I'm really tired. But I need to check the footage from my camera at the warehouse. I don't have fucking Alfred to do this shit for me.

I start reviewing. It's boring as shit. I fast forward, because I just want Davis. In the back of my mind, I'm debating reporting his car as stolen, just to annoy him. But that might give something away to him.

I'm watching, bored, but at about four in the afternoon, I noticed the camera gets . . . gauzy. If that's a word. Like I'm filming underwater.

Then I realize what's happened.

A bird shit on it.

The bird either shit on the top of the camera, or on the pole, and the shit slowly leaked down and covered the lens.

By six, it had hardened, and I can't see shit after that.

God damn it.

I texted Olivia around midnight. She'd just finished up and was having dinner with the theater owner, so she just said don't wait up.

For a few minutes, I debated my move. I was tired. I'd had kickboxing and outcalls today . . . but I hated Davis more than I was tired. I got my Cube gear together and headed to the warehouse.

Once there, I scaled the roof and found my shit-covered bug. I had brought a very small piece of plywood, a spare bookshelf for one of the bookcases I have at home. Not that I read, but I put plants in the bookcases. Anyhow, I set it up on the cover of the air vent, with about a two-inch hangover. That wouldn't block anything important, 'cause I wasn't bugging the fucking sky. But it should keep the birds off. I zip tied it in place.

Using my phone, I checked the angles, everything looked good. The warehouse on this night appeared closed, nobody there, so there was no point hanging around. I went home and decided to get a good night's sleep. After all, I was a working girl.

Chapter Eight
Insurance Games

Insurance executives pay well, so when this CEO at Black Rock Insurance called Nina, she went to me for the appointment. Normally on Thursday I'm evenings and nights, but I was available and not doing shit but watching the warehouse camera and wondering if Davis would ever come back.

I liked the gig. I'm somewhat of a pragmatic hero . . . I'm quite willing to take big money from corporations and funnel it back to the girls at the shelter . . . well, and Steve Madden for new shoes. I'm like Robin Hood if he had to dress like a hooker.

Anyhow, I dressed for the part, wearing black dress pants, a formal sky-blue blouse, and a black jacket. To offset, white purse and heels. For style, I wore a gold necklace and pink earrings. Pink blush, mascara, and a royal blue hairband rounded out my ensemble. I was somewhat impressed. I looked like a Vice-President.

Of course, that was always something I was good at. One of the first lessons I learned at the agency was never look the part. Look better. Look classy. If you do, no one gives you a second look.

Their home office was a huge black skyscraper near the Spaghetti Bowl, which for you non-locals is this giant conglomeration of freeways that came together on the northwest side of town. The 15, the 515, the 93, the 95, and MLK Boulevard all come together in a giant mess . . . and people wonder why there's always traffic here.

Idiots.

Anyhow, the building wasn't owned entirely by Black Rock. They leased the seventh through the top floor of the sixteen-story building. The penthouse offices for the big-wigs was on the sixteenth floor, naturally.

I checked in with security in the lobby, my heels echoing on the clean tile floor. The place was typical insurance; brown, gray, white, stuffy and clean. Reception gave me a guest badge, then I took a private elevator to floor sixteen. I had no idea what they insured, nor did I fucking care. All I cared was that they were solvent and therefore the money would be good.

There I met the secretary, or personal assistant, or whatever they're called these days. She reminded me a little of me — blue on blonde, black dress, pretty face, decent body. She eyed me as if I were worm roadkill and icily pointed to a large white sofa to wait. A redone version of some Bruce Springsteen tune floated through the air and made me want to kill myself. I pretended to play on my phone. Miss Stuffy said nothing else and either worked hard or pretended to work hard.

"Miss Starlight, pleased. Howard Cochoran, CEO. Come in," he said as he came through the open door.

I rose and eyed him. He had a scarred face, probably one of those kids that itched chicken pox, which he hid behind a beard. Receding hair, a bit overweight but not bad, probably in his fifties. Expensive suit, wedding ring, and piercing blue eyes.

I shook his hand. "Nice to meet you, Mr. Cochoran."

"Howard, please. Just not Howie."

I smiled, my winning smile. "Sure. I'm Shelby."

We entered his office, which was the size of an ocean liner and had a great view of the traffic stacked up on the 515. The walls were lined with insurance tomes, the bookshelf behind his desk with pictures. The room was off-center. The larger area to the right had a putting green.

Golf. Yuck.

"Nice green," I said, sitting in a luxurious chair in front of his desk. He obviously had just cleaned. The room smelled like lemon Pledge.

"Thanks. You play?"

Smiling politely, I said, "Not so much."

"A shame. Well, would you like a drink? Snack?"

"I'm good, really. I'm curious why you called me for this assignment, to be frank. You must have a much cheaper, go-to girl that could handle something like this," I said.

He smiled. "I like your . . . auxiliary talents. Barry Davidson recommended you highly."

Okay, *now* I got it — Davidson was a regular client. He was a cocaine cowboy and always had a lot of cash, but I earned it 'cause the coke kept him from, shall we say, performing efficiently.

Smiling sexily, I said, "Any friend of Barry is a friend of mine."

"Rates?"

"Insurance or mine?" I asked.

He smiled. "Yours."

"Make an offer," I said.

Five thousand.

"Multiply by two and we're on."

We were on.

During the time between banging Cochoran and officially being on-call, I did laundry, I went grocery shopping, and I did some stretches. I checked the camera and noticed that the warehouse seemed closed. There wasn't jackshit going on. Still, that wasn't too abnormal for a lot of shipping places in the middle of the day. They tended to boom or bust around whenever shipments came in, which could be any time of the day or night.

But I did decide I'd better take a cruise by overnight after my last call as the Cube and check it out. A full day of total inactivity was just odd enough to bear investigation.

This covert stuff isn't what I really like about being the Cube. As the Cube, my main objective is to shut down totem users or really extreme scumbags the law can't touch, like serial killers that eat people, like that fuck in New Mexico last week. After all, that's not something the ordinary cop can achieve. And Sam Grant, when he used to be in charge, would occasionally post interesting stuff on my website. Medina does that, too. They like to help me without helping, y'know?

But my site, which like I said Olivia handles, basically gets me a lot of attention and some leads outside the norm. I mean, people post for incredibly stupid shit for a super-hero. I mean, do you need a superheroine to get your wife's wedding ring out of the drain or shovel your sidewalk if it snows in Montana? Get a fucking clue, people.

However, a lot of domestic abuse stuff shows up. Olivia showed me some of it once, and I told her I never want to see it again. For one thing, it just made me think of being nearly raped back in the day. For another, there were a ton of them, *wayyyyyyy* to many for me to handle. Even if that was all I did all day. And third, that fact broke my heart. Olivia's tougher than I am.

But she did pass the occasional request to me, and it was usually something where the woman had no chance of winning. Such a request came from Diane Coffey of Henderson a while back. Diane was this blue eyed blonde from Maryland or somewhere back east who met the love of her life on a summer vacation after senior year and married him six weeks later. That was ten years ago. Now she had a six- and eight-year-old, while he was a major player with the WSA in Vegas. He also liked to cheat on her and beat her when the mood struck him, about once a month or so. She wanted to leave, but she was smart enough to know with the WSA, he'd know everything about her.

Olivia showed this to me at a Taco Bell and I inadvertently channeled earth and ruptured the booth and the table. What the hell, they have insurance, but we did get out of there quick.

I knew I had to be cautious approaching Diane, make sure Mike the Soldier boy didn't pick me up. I watched his place and found out he was doing a liaison with Nellis Air Force base. That helped. I waited for a day when her kids were busy playing the backyard of their home then I approached dressed as the Cube. I just knocked on the fucking door.

She opened it and her eyes grew wide.

"I'm here to help. Can I come in?"

She nodded quickly. She was probably once very pretty with a round face, freckles, blue eyes, and curly blonde hair that was a bit of a mess right now. She was wearing a white blouse and faded jeans with yellow gloves and had been mopping the floor. Her weight was a little heavy, but not bad, typical of early thirties mom types.

"You . . . you really came," she said.

I smiled. "Sure."

The kitchen was cheap and all kid-oriented, with crayon drawings stuck everywhere and Ikea cabinets. The dining room table had scratches on the legs and surface. Some were obviously from a compass. I didn't even know kids were given those things anymore. I thought they were considered weapons.

"I . . . have a seat."

I sat and said, "I don't want to stay long. I know your husband is at Nellis, but even so, it's best to keep this on the down low."

"I agree. Can you help me?"

"I think so, but what do you want?"

"I just want him to go and know that if he hassles me or Jimmy or Jean that . . . you know . . . I can fight back."

I nodded. I saw this story posted on my site tons of times, or more accurately, Olivia saw it and told me about it. Like I said, I kept a distance from the site.

"I can deliver a message," I said. "But I can't make him listen. I've been where you are. I know how hopeless it feels, so I'm gonna try."

"That's . . . thank you," she said, and she kissed me on the cheek.

I actually blushed, me the call girl.

Delivering the message was pretty easy. Mike the solider boy had a favorite bar, a country and western type of place. I waited until he was finished, hanging out around his black Ford F350 pickup.

When he came out, he wasn't drunk. He moved to get in the truck, and I stepped in front in full Kevlar and mask.

"What the fuck? Hey, I'm not in the mood, lady."

I grabbed him by the shirt and slammed him against the truck as I said, "I'm here from Diane. She's leaving you, and you're going to agree to terms and leave her alone, or this will happen again."

Smirking at me, he said, "You gotta be kidding. I'm WSA. I'm going to knock your fucking teeth in."

I headbutted him, then moved and put an electrical taser into his gut. This wasn't the kind that knocks people out or stops them from moving. This was basically a hand-held cattle prod.

God, I love the fucking internet. Oh, and bondage play. That's what this thing was actually for, which makes me glad I stay away from that stuff and limit my kinky side to anal sex and eating cum off the floor, shit like that.

He yelped and dropped hard, because I'd kicked him in the balls with an iron-toed boot, one of my many weapons. Once he was down, I kicked him again. He didn't fight back, because he was busy crying.

I grabbed his hair and said, "Got the picture, Mikey?"

"G . . . got it," he grunted.

"I'm watching her every day. One wrong move, any retaliation, and you're going to be cooked like morning bacon."

"Got it. Don't use that thing again."

I honestly couldn't believe what a pussy he was. He didn't even make a second try at me. Not that it would've worked, but I expected him to try.

I got a message back to Diane with a simple phone call. She was grateful. I told her to post that to my site. She still posts updates from Maryland or wherever she moved back to. Nice.

Sometimes, it's good to be a superheroine.

Anyhow, enough of that. I had a call about seven. It's a training call, me and a TS. Agency wants to scope her out. I'm game for that. I kind'a like it, y'know, me, a mentor.

Shows you how fucked up this business is.

Forty minutes later I'm meeting Brenda the TS in the hallway of the average type of hotel room at, well, it was an average place. I'm honest, here, I'm a little surprised I had a job at the Palace Station. They weren't the ritz. The Empire's type of clients usually took bigger places. Now, possibly this was an old-timer deal, or it was maybe someone who knew someone who ran the hotel. Turned out to be the latter. Still, I was surprised, but what the fuck, you go where the job takes you.

I like Brenda, who is tall with long, straight brown hair, a nice body, good makeup and hair. Chest is artificial, of course, but well done. She's wearing a white blouse and black skirt with nylons and blue heels. I'm wearing sandals, red short-shots, and a slutty white camisole, as per the customer's request. I'm dressed so hooker I almost look like a parody of a hooker.

"Hi, Shelby. You're Brenda?" I asked, holding out a hand. Her fingernails are pink, hands are really clean and moist.

"Yes, nice to meet you," she says with a nod.

"Look, I know this is the first time, but it's easy, don't worry. Just follow my lead. You get in a spot where you don't know what's going on, just say it's your birthday and I'll take the lead."

She smiled. "Sure, that's great. I'm nervous."

"We all are the first time. That's cool. Nerves are good," I say with a wink. "You from around here?"

"Danville, Illinois."

"Whoa. How old are you?"

"Twenty-three."

"Nice. Okay, I'll be honest, I'm about your age, I'm from Fullerton, which is a suburb of LA. Moved to Vegas at eighteen and I've been getting butt-banged since." That made her laugh, which was good. "Anyhow, this'll be fun. Just stay cool."

I reached in and kissed her. After, I said, "The guys almost always want that. You're a good kisser, but yeah, you're nervous."

"Sorry."

"Don't be. We were all rookies once."

Yeah, Brenda *does* remind me of *my* first outcall way back in the fuckin' day. So back then, I'm the newbie, and I'm teamed with this freckled redhead named Angie, who is still in the business, but she moved to Miami. Anyhow, it's two guys who are business partners who closed a major deal and want to celebrate.

I'm nervous as shit, not about the sex, but you know, all the other stuff. Angie told me three simple rules. "Follow my lead, get the money first, and just be yourself."

"Right."

We go into this hotel room, which at the time looked fancy and exotic, but now probably looks boring. Anyhow, two guys are there, a blond and a brown-haired dude, both these sort of yeasty, pale-faced Midwestern types with glasses who look like, well, businesspeople. Think IT or accounting types. They look pretty nervous as well.

Angie takes the lead and blond guy likes me. Once I got into the chit-chat and asked about this business and all, Angie was right, I just had to be myself. Everything was fine.

They wanted some oral and then a good fuck.

This was when I learned I was not great at the ol' BJ, especially with a condom. It's like sucking a pacifier. This threw me off. Luckily, the guy thought I was the best-looking woman he'd ever had, and I probably was, so he went with it. But I knew I sucked at sucking.

The sex was fine. He let me lead, which worked, and it wasn't long and really made him happy.

Afterwards, I asked Angie, "How do I learn to blow properly?"

She shrugged. "Practice."

I wasn't thrilled with that advice. What the fuck was I going to do, wander bars and shopping malls and ask guys, "Wanna go back and get a blow job so I can learn to do it right?"

Fortunately, I stumbled into a solution by accident. I was given the green light to go solo by my fourth call, and on my fifth call I came down to the lobby of the Excalibur and saw someone I knew. She'd been at the agency when I interviewed. Nina's agency is into everything: guys, TS, TV, women. Just no dogs or kids. Anyhow, there was this good-looking TS named Mary who had long black hair, nice rack, nice butt. I mean, top of the line. She was sitting in a chair texting on her phone, wearing a blue blouse and white pants, looking like a business person.

I went up to her. I was wearing a ponytail and a tennis outfit. Hey, it met the client's fantasies. "Hey, girl."

She smiled. "I remember you. You were in a little while ago for an interview. Shelly?"

"Close. Shelby."

I shook her head. Then she asked, "How's it going?"

"I'm doing great." Then I leaned down and whispered, "But can you teach me how to suck cock?"

She laughed. "Seriously? That's *all* you need to learn?"

"That's it," I said with a smile.

She stood and hugged me, then said, "I like your moxie, girl. I have a call now. But tomorrow, I have a day off. You call me and I'll teach you how to blow any cock this side of the Mississippi."

I laughed. "Okay. Where are you from?"

"Philadelphia. You?"

"Fullerton. LA."

"Got it. We'll make this a bicoastal blow job training session."

So, the next day, I met her. We had Starbucks and she talked about her miserable childhood being bullied and picked on. She turned eighteen, came to Vegas, had surgery, and never looked back. I told her about my mom. She missed her parents. They had supported her. It was the society at large that drove her to the land of . . . well, whatever the fuck Vegas is the land of. The land of opportunity, I guess.

She taught me how to suck. I learned a blow job isn't a blow job, it's more of a hand-suck job. This accomplishes a lot. One, it's faster. Stroking the guy while sucking the head is more stimulation. Two, it's easier with a guy with a condom and a way to make sure the condom is holding up. And believe me, not all condoms are created equal. Three, be patient. As I've made clear, I'm in this for the money. I have no desire to spent eight minutes blowing some freemason from Kansas City if I can do it in two and get the fuck outta there, unless he happens to be entertaining. Which isn't often. I like making people happy and talking, but most of these guys are just using me as a therapist.

She also taught me to be aggressive. I thought a guy's dick was like a clit, like super-sensitive, but it's not. Well, the non-circumcised guys are a little different, but they're not that common. Anyhow, I was too gentle. You gotta get traction and pressure.

Anyhow, I paid her for the lesson, and we still get together every so often and shop costumes. Mary is a blast. We even went to a show at one of the hotels. I don't remember much about that one. I got stone-faced fucking drunk and just remember it was fun. I'm not big into drinking, but I was that night. Whoooo!

Back to whatever the fuck I was talking about.

Oh, yeah, outcall with Brenda. This was a piece of cake. The guy had never been with a TS. I pegged him as a repressed gay, you know, the type that wanted a man but couldn't risk that, but somehow getting banged by a girl was okay. Men are, as I may have said, fragile and fucked up creatures.

Brenda did well. I text the agency and let them know they have a winner, and chatted with her a bit in the lobby over a drink. She tells me about the prejudice in Smallville, or wherever the fuck I said she was from. Rough. I have learned that I was lucky being raised in Fullerton. Lots of people east of, say, the California border are raised with seriously fucked up heads.

So, after my two outcalls, it's about midnight. I race home, switch into Cube costume, grab a diet Coke, and head out. I get to the warehouse rooftop at 12:42.

Then I watch birds try to shit on me for an hour and listen to crickets.

Okay, that's not quite right. There's no birds out at night, though I'm sure if there had been they would have been shitting on me. And there were noises other than crickets. And mostly, I played around on my phone.

But the net result of this is simple. Nothing. No lights, no traffic, no nothing.

I give up at two. I head home, take a very quick shower, and flop into bed at 2:28 in a turquoise camisole and white panties.

End of story.

Not so much.

"Wake up!"

I wake up and start to scream, but a hand clamps over my mouth.

A cold hand.

I'm instantly awake, grabbing my attacker and throwing him off, recognizing him as I do so.

"Woody!"

I acted as if attacked by a human — logically, one usually expects someone attacking you in your bed at night to be a man and most certainly a human. Well, unless you're me. Anyhow, Woody lands hard against the closet doors, and I'm leaping out of bed before he can move.

"You're dead, you knothole!" I shout, and I get my hands on his neck and squeeze.

"I don't breathe, ya dumb blonde! This is an emergency! Davis is on the move!"

That stops me dead, much more effectively than any attack. I just stare at him, and if he had wanted to hurt me, he could've killed me. I was that stunned.

"Davis! Moving! *Now*! You still understand English?" he shouted, grabbing a pair of gray track pants with a red stripe that were lying on my futon and throwing them at me.

I shake my head. "What? What? How do you know about Davis? How did you get out?"

Woody's features were frozen, of course, but I could tell he was rolling his eyes mentally as he said, "I'm a marionette. I just slipped out an air vent and killed a few roaches on the way. My books are fakes, kid. No one reads <u>The Odyssey</u> except English majors, and even they cheat. I've got a computer inside it. And a phone."

I stand up and put my hands on my hips, glad I never sleep in the nude — exactly because of stupid situations like this. "Wait. Look, I don't need you. I know where Davis is. I was just keeping you in the storage locker because Olivia seems to like you and I was checking out your story, but Davis is under surveillance."

He slapped his forehead. "Yeah, I've seen you, kid. I've got a drone that watches all that. You're so 1999."

I was pissed at being invaded and insulted . . . maybe not even in that order. "Go eat a termite."

Imploring me with a wringing of his hands, he said, "Can you please put on your pants or bat-cape or whatever and *let's go*. He's clearing out the place!"

Suddenly, I could see he was serious, so the shock immediately wore off. Noticing the clock, it was 4:14, still dark. I grabbed my Kevlar off the counter and said, "Okay."

I dressed as fast as I could.

"Hurry up! Jesus H. Christ, blondie! I could work a Rubik's cube faster than this!"

"Hey, this shit isn't like putting on pants, ya know. It's worse than a fucking corset." As I secured it, I glared at him sitting on my bed and said, "How fucking old are you anyhow? What's a Rubik's cube?"

"I'll explain on the way. You gotta drive."

I put on my mask. "Well, sure. Your short ass isn't reaching any pedals."

The drive to the warehouse took only nine minutes with me driving. On the way, Woody explained he saw Davis arrive on the drone at 3:34, so well after I left and much later than he had ever arrived before. Woody watched a few minutes and realized he and a couple cronies were quickly taking boxes out of the warehouse and loading them into a black Sprinter that looked like a second-hand Amazon delivery van with all the logos stripped off. Once he got out, he called his drone and rode it to my place, so he didn't know what had happened since that time.

"You should have more drones," I said.

"Hey, they cost a lot. Tell your girlfriend to make more money and I'll buy more."

"You paid for them with *her money*?" I asked with a glare.

"Er, uh, that's a long story," he said guiltily. "It's not exactly like I can get a credit card, and y'know, she doesn't pay me!"

I slapped the back of his head. "You two can discuss this after this shit is over."

When we got close, I parked and we went to the rooftop to spy, knowing that spot was secure. I used binoculars and could see they were almost done. There were three big vans, all the sort of Sprinter than Amazon uses for their fleet, though these were just plain black vans. A fourth vehicle was parked near our right side, the left of the back, near the driveway. It was parked oddly parallel to the driveway. It was one of those giant douche trucks. It had huge dual tires, all this chrome trapping, some sort of Ford 3500 series, the back end fully loaded. It was shiny red.

Davis was working hard. He wore a gray hoodie, jeans, and boots. He was mostly pointing at shit on the dock and to the vans, barking orders like a Nazi movie leftover. The other three were in their vans, which were backed up to the dock in the middle, so beyond his truck. I couldn't see the well. They wore black hoodies and pants. I could tell from the movements two were women, one a man.

"Fuck," I muttered.

"I assume you're cursing and not ordering me to do something that's impossible for a man made of wood."

"Fuck as in they're almost done. Look."

I handed him the binoculars and bit my lip, worried. The last few boxes were going in. They were typical storage bins, but one had a blue lid.

"Damn. That one with the blue lid is the key. It's full of totems."

I took the binoculars and suddenly caught my breath. I saw something horrible. There was a young girl with stringy black hair, braces, and freckles sitting in the front of the Ford. Because it was parked parallel, she was easy to see. Wearing a black hoodie, she had her head down and was handcuffed to a rollbar inside the cab.

"Motherfucker," I hissed.

"What's wrong?" asked Woody.

"You know that girl that went missing after soccer practice last night?"

"Yeah."

"That's her down there. Rosa Rodriguez."

"Shit."

I put down the binoculars and said, "I've got to stop them. I can't let them take the kid. Stay here and call Olivia if anything goes wrong."

"I'm not fucking Alfred. I can help!"

"How? By giving them splinters? I'll be back," I said, then I took off fast.

I was furious, although under control. I wasn't angry for me, right now, but for this girl. I could only guess what horrors he'd done to her. He was not leaving this property alive, that much I fucking knew.

They had security off because they were moving. Fast. Fuck, they even left the front gate open. I slipped inside and moved to the back. My gear blended in well, but I wasn't exactly invisible. However, I was counting on them being in a rush.

Davis' truck was parked just to the corner. With luck, I could use the front of the cab for cover, then slide between the truck and warehouse and attack. I couldn't take time to free Rosa first. I could easily free her once Davis and his three workers were down. There were four of them. If they all had paranormal powers, I was in for a battle. But I didn't sense any aural blockers, and I only sensed power in Davis. I had to strike fast, like a teenage boy shooting while jacking off.

I moved cautiously. Davis had his back to me. The other three were in the van. I was about to channel earth hard and rip up the parking lot under his feet, throwing him into the air and into the building.

Didn't get the chance.

"Cowabungaaaaaaaaaaaaaaaaaaaaaaa!"

"What the fuck? Aghhhhhhhhhhhhhhhhh!"

I stood still, shocked as Woody jumped from the roof of the warehouse armed with a butcher's knife, aiming right for Davis. Davis was, quite understandably, shocked shitless. He just stood there as Woody hit him like a flying bowling ball, stabbed him in the chest, and rolled off from the impact.

I was about to move when Rosa shrieked, "No! No, he's hurting my dad!"

"*Dad*?" I asked, stunned.

"Daddy!" she shrieked, crying.

In an instant, Davis went from being a kidnapping douche bag fuckface scumbag TM to . . . just a guy. All my rage for him was . . . gone. That sucked. It was more fun hating him.

That instant passed fast, because I instantly realized I didn't have to worry about her. She wasn't a victim, she was just out working with dad, sort of. I moved fast. I raced towards Woody and Davis, channeling earth to drive Davis, who was yelling and bleeding like a stuck pig, into the back of the dock.

This inadvertently blew Woody across the parking lot.

Unfortunately, our battle with Davis gave the other three a few seconds to leap into the vans and haul ass. I couldn't let Davis get away. As I approached Davis laying on the dock, I saw he was out cold. I checked his vitals, and he was weak.

Woody came over and shouted, "Free the girl!"

"*He's her dad*!" I shouted, nodding towards Rosa, who was still cuffed in the truck.

"He's . . . what?"

Angry at myself more than him, I took it out on him. What the fuck. He can deal with it. I shoved a hand into his chest and said, "You are not a fucking hero!"

This was now a major league shitstorm, because I had a 14-year-old girl that had just seen her father skewered by a marionette aiding the Cube. I quickly pulled out my phone and called 9-1-1.

"This is the Cube at a warehouse, 3775 E. Sunset. I've got a man who had a fight with his buddies and got stabbed. He's weak but stable. Please hurry."

Then I hung up and grabbed Woody. "Come on, fuck face. Not a word of this to anyone ever. You asshole. I had him set up to blow into the warehouse. I had it all handled!"

"Sorry," he said, and I think he genuinely was. "Wait."

He pulled some metal gizmo from his pocket that looked like the remote control for a drone. Then he flipped a switch and said, "Electronic scrambler. No one here is going to see anything, unless they back the footage real time into the cloud, which is doubtful for a shithole like this."

"Good work. Let's roll."

We took off. Chasing the vans was impossible. They had a huge head start, and we were just a few blocks from the 15. They'd be in fucking Utah by the time we started after them.

The ambulance moved fucking fast. We got to my car. Woody had to hide in the trunk. I the on a sweatshirt over the Kevlar and yanked off my mask, tossing it on the floorboard. Then I calmly pulled into traffic, meeting an ambulance and cop car heading the other way.

I was shaking. I couldn't believe how knowing Davis was a father changed *everything*. I felt horrible for Rosa. We had gone there to stop him, and instead she watched us skewer him.

I was just hoping the cops would ignore her blathering about a crazy doll stabbing her after and think she was hysterical. I mean, fuck, if I was a cop, I would.

Unfortunately, Woody's rash attack also blew any chance we had of getting information out of Davis, or the warehouse, anything. The only thing I had were the plates for the vans.

Once we got home, I got Woody out of the trunk and he immediately said, "I really fucked up bad. I'm sorry. I just lost it. You have no idea how much he hurt my friends . . . separated me from my sister. I lost it."

I wanted to punch him, but I understood his anger at Davis. Shit. I would have done the same if I were a piece of wood and not a sexy hooker.

I just said, "It's done. Let's figure out how to find Davis' posse. Logically, if Davis was going with them — and since he had his daughter, he certainly was — they likely were heading for Flannagan for some reason. The others may know where Flannagan is."

"Yeah . . . yeah, could be. But where are they?"

"Dunno. I have the plates, but I don't know if that helps. Do something useful and turn on the news. We should keep an eye out and see if there's news of the battle."

"Forget that! This is an emergency!"

I threw him inside the door after unlocking it. "Well, thanks to you, *we have no leads*!"

He was silent a moment, then said, "Good point."

"I know. Sit there and figure something out. I'll shower and see if *I* can figure something out. In this partnership, I'm the fucking brains."

Chapter Nine
Tahoe
Friday, April 2, 2021

"That wasn't smart," said Medina.

"No fucking shit."

I was sitting at the table in a white terrycloth robe with my hair in a towel eating a bagel with cream cheese. Woody was watching the TV. I had showered and called Medina, swallowing my pride and asking her to track the plates like some second-rate P.I.

Of course, this had a drawback. She wanted to know why I wanted the plate info. Imagine that! Anyhowwwww . . . after a highly edited version of our battle, where I explained my new partner accidentally skewered Davis and he and his kid were left at the scene, Medina made her comment.

"So, you think these totem runners are in the vans with these plates? It would make sense. They're registered to the corporation that runs the warehouse at the address you gave me."

"Yep, makes sense. I gotta find 'em."

"Is it personal?"

"No. I mean, I don't even know who they fucking are," I said with exasperation. "Look, can you help or not?"

"I'll help," said Medina quickly. "I was hoping to get a field agent to help you. I'm keying up the plates now . . . last hit is a little while back, they picked up on a stoplight on the 95 at Nellis Air Force Base."

"That's weird."

"Why is that?" asked Medina.

Medina was from Maine. She'd only been running Ops in Vegas for like a couple months or so, you know, local geography wasn't really her strong point. "There's not shit out there after Nellis until you get up to Tahoe."

"Oh. I can probably get a paranormal agent to Tahoe by tomorrow."

Look, I was willing to take help, especially now that Davis was under wraps. But I didn't want to get sucked into being part of an Ops operation. "I don't think it's worth it. I mean, where are they going and why? These guys are minnows, Medina. Davis was the big fish, and he's caught. Don't waste an agent."

"Good point," she said, but I wasn't sure if that was sarcasm or agreement.

"Can you keep me posted on the plates?" I asked, eager to change the subject and close the call.

"I can run a search loop and it will alert me, so sure. But there's not much in the way of cameras in the woods."

"Well, I'm going to Tahoe," I said, and Woody immediately turned to me. "They have to be going there if they're past Nellis, so I might as well get a head start."

"That sounds reasonable."

"Thanks. I'll send you some candy or some shit."

"Shelby."

I winced. She had "mom" voice.

"Yes, Miss Kane?"

"For what it's worth, there's no contact at all from Vegas PD. If they contact me . . . I'll smooth things over."

For this, I was very grateful. It's nice to have friends. Sometimes. "I appreciate it. I'll talk to my puppet buddy. This shit won't happen again."

"Good. Isn't he a zombie marionette?"

"Uh, yeah. Oh, and let me know if the kid is okay."

"Sure. We'll stay in touch."

I hung up and Woody looked at me. "Puppet buddy?"

I slapped him on the head. "Shut up. You're on the shit list. We start booking flights for Tahoe while I call Olivia. I'll explain later."

"I got the gist of it."

"Okay." He toddled off the bedroom to use the laptop while I dialed Olivia.

"Shelby, this better be important," she muttered.

"It is," I said seriously.

I knew I had her attention then. She said, "Sorry. I didn't get in until after two. What's wrong?"

"Trouble. Davis is down, but his cronies got away and are headed your way. Woody and I are on the way up."

"Huh? *What*? Dial back."

I just said, "I'll explain later. Woody helped me put Davis down, and we can use him. We'll be up there by lunchtime. Let's have lunch and I'll explain."

She was quiet a minute, then said, "I can handle lunch. Until then I'm going back to bed. You okay?"

"I'm fine. Just pissed these guys got away."

Confidently, she said, "We'll get 'em. See you for lunch."

Woody rode cargo. He didn't like it, but fuck him. I watched the news all the way to Tahoe, which is a real short flight. We got there about ten. I checked into a Ramada Inn near the airport.

The news coverage of Davis' capture was unusually quiet. Davis was in a custody dispute with his wife, so kidnapping the girl to go on the run wasn't seen as much of a stretch. It was simply noted he appeared to have been injured in a fight between drug gangs at his warehouse and was under arrest. Rosa seemed fine. I saw a thirty second clip of her being returned home. Her Hispanic mom was fat and sad looking, crying with relief.

There was not one word on any news feed about the Cube. So, either Rosa left that out or the cops ignored her . . . or they contacted Medina and kept their mouth shut about paranormal shit, including knife-wielding puppets. Marionettes.

That was a relief. That was a complication I didn't need, because not long after I checked in, Medina called with bad news.

"The vans were found dumped near a Burger King in Carson City," said Medina. "No cameras in the area."

"Shit. Well, I'd hide my tracks if I ate at Burger King, too."

"The van was wiped of prints. The van was registered to the warehouse. We have some DNA samples, but those take time to process."

"Great. Fuck me sideways," I muttered.

"I'd rather not," said Medina. "We have people at the airports. I asked the NSA for help. But your description is really vague, and unless they are paranormal and pop up on apps detectors, I don't think we'll get them."

"I don't think they're leaving. I don't see why they'd drive here if they didn't have to transport something here," I said. "I mean, if they were gonna fly, just fly out of Vegas. Or even take a train. They gotta be doing something in this fuckdump town."

"Valid argument, though I'm not sure the fine citizens of Carson City or even Tahoe would consider their town a fuckdump. What can I do?"

"Nothing yet. Olivia and I have a lunch date. Maybe she'll have some ideas."

"I do have an idea, but it's out there," said Olivia as she sucked down the last of her diet Coke. She'd eaten enough to feed a horse. She never ate before shows, and she'd been in bed with the manager the night before, so she was starving.

"I'm all ears," I said as we sat at a Denny's off the 395.

"Me, too," said Woody.

Olivia slapped him with a spoon and hissed, "Shut up, idiot. You're a marionette!"

"If someone sees me talking, then you'll have to mime that you're making me talk, like a ventriloquist," he muttered.

She sighed. She was wearing leggings that were zebra-striped, a blue shirt, and a black hoodie. Woody was wearing a tux. Hey, I thought he should dress for success. I was wearing white pants, a red shirt with black vertical stripes, a black hairband, and white sneakers. I looked about as un-hooker-like as possible, more like casual co-ed.

"So let's have the idea, BFF. This is no time for stupid ideas, because termite-head over there and I have come up with zero plus jackshit, which equals nothing."

"I didn't know hookers could do math," said Woody sarcastically.

I glared at him. "I own a drill, y'know."

Olivia wasn't joining us. She looked concerned, and she stirred her diet Coke with the straw. Then she said, "Necromancy isn't just . . . magic from the dead."

"Everyone knows that," said Woody.

She ignored him and looked at me. "Do you think Davis and his people killed anyone?"

"I wouldn't bet against it. He kidnapped his own kid and me. I'd say anger management is not his forte, and lack of control leads to dumb things like, say, whapping someone on the head with a tire iron."

She nodded.

"Olivia . . . you seem really upset. I mean, what is this about?"

Looking at me hard, she said, "Communicating with the dead is the other part. Look, I know we've talked briefly about this. It's not like I can just talk to any dead people. But there's a lot of people that are sort of dead but in-between. Everyone has a short transition period of life to death. But some souls . . . usually traumatized or betrayed souls . . . they linger. They can linger for centuries."

"You think someone Davis crossed before might be within reach?" I asked with obvious skepticism. Well, shit, I was. I mean, who wouldn't be?

"Yes."

Woody said, "That's a longshot. I mean, I've heard of this, but without a specific tie to the deceased or the target, it's probably not gonna happen. We've got better odds of finding them by conventional means. They had to change vehicles. The cops will find out where they are, then we move in."

I shook my head. "No, we give it a try, provided your up to it, Olivia. Is this hard?"

Shrugging, she said, "It's more of a pain in the ass." She sipped the last of her diet Coke and said, "Let's give it a shot. We need somewhere private and, uh, Andy may still be at my hotel room."

I nodded. Hey, Olivia slept with guys on the road. She had no problems making someone who could help her career happy. I realize a lot of women would have a problem with that, but the reality is, that's reality in show biz. So, get off your high-horse. Women have been sleeping their way to the top since mankind crawled outta the mud or swung down from trees or God created us or whatever.

"We have a place," said Woody.

"Then let's roll. There's no reason to wait. The sooner we find them, the sooner we can shut them down."

We met at the hotel twenty minutes later. When Olivia entered, she asked me, "Are you okay as the Cube, or has the girl yapped?"

"I dunno, but I haven't heard anything bad yet."

Olivia put her purse on the bed. "Well, your social medica accounts are all quiet as well. That's good news."

"Yeah. Okay, what do we do?"

Olivia said, "This is a little tricky. Usually when performing the contact channeling, I'm in the place where the person I want died. I'm not. And usually, I know who I want to talk to. But this time, I don't. I'm kind of like a fisherman casting a giant net. I might find what I want or find a bunch of, like, diapers and other trash. Or a shark."

"Shark?" asked Woody with alarm.

"Not all the dead are . . . gentle," she said. "I ran across one seriously fucked up ghost a few months ago."

"You never told me this," I said, now very worried.

She smiled. "Relax. It's okay. I'm just saying . . . anyhow, we all want to talk, so let's sit on the floor cross-legged and in a triangle, and whoever manifests should appear above us."

"We *are* in a hotel," pointed out Woody. "If this gets loud or showy, we'll be in deep shit."

"It won't," said Olivia definitely. "Unless you're a baby and shit your pants."

"Impossible. I'm made of wood."

She winked at me. "Then we're good. Let's assemble."

We moved quickly into position. As we prepared, Olivia said, "One last thing. Keep physical contact. Breaking the link will cause the ghost to dissipate."

"Got it," I said.

"I knew *that*," said Woody.

Olivia nodded and shut her eyes. She mumbled a bit, then said something in Spanish. I don't know any language other than English. Well, I know hooker English, which is a kind of second language. Anyhow, a thick green mist slowly filled the room.

"Uh, Olivia, its . . . foggy."

"Ignore it. Concentrate. *I'm getting someone!*" she said, looking at us with excitement in her eyes. She looked like a girl getting her first vibrator.

Then we suddenly see something forming between us, and the mist is so thick we can't see the walls of the hotel room. I'm *not* excited. I'm ready to wet myself, because this is nerve wracking. Hey, I can handle rapists and TMs and even farting during sex, but talking with the dead is messing with a trouble of a whole different color, you know?

Then in the mist I see a figure.

Whooooooooooooaaaaaaaaaaa.

It's a woman . . . I think. Yeah, it's a woman. Imagine a woman with short-cut but full, brown hair, brown eyes, and a pretty face but a big jaw. You know, like women in Nebraska or somewhere. Average looks, average body, sort of your girl-next-door type, except the type that doesn't turn into a hot anal sex nymphomaniac like in a porn film. She's maybe a little tall.

But . . . there's two *weird* things. First is she's naked, which I guess isn't weird. Ghosts don't need clothes. But second, her head is, well, upside-down. That's the only way to put it. Imagine someone ripped off your head and stuck it back on your neck upside down and welded it in place. That's exactly the look. There's a suture mark where the flesh was joined, and the top of her head has tendons, veins, and her spine sticking out.

I turn around and barf. Remember, I'm the girl who was licking cum off some guy's shoes in a hotel a few days ago, and I immediately barf, so you know how gross this is to look at.

Olivia seems unfazed by this. She stares at the woman in the center of our triangle and asks breathlessly, "Who are you?"

The woman speaks in a sad tone. "I'm Barbra Morris of San Jose."

"When did ya kick it?" asked Woody just before Olivia can ask another question. Me, I'm not into the conversation. I'm busy wiping barf off my face.

"In 1972. I am here because the need is urgent, and I have not yet passed on. I remain in limbo, between life and death, seeking to warn others of my fate."

"Less melodrama and more facts, lady. Not to sound rude, but you're not on a time clock and we are. We're trying to save people," said Olivia.

"I was turned into this horror by evil people. They now plan to use another victim to bring back one from Hell, a powerful TM killed years ago. The unwilling victim of the sacrifice will wind up . . . as I am."

"Dead."

"Trapped in limbo, after a horrific, gruesome death caused by Soloman's Liquid and ritual torture and sacrifice," she said.

I finally had my sea legs, so to speak, and said, "I don't want anyone to wind up like you."

She looked at me. I almost barfed again. Morris said, "Wise."

Olivia said, "We know the need is urgent. But we don't know where to go."

Morris chuckled, which was a little disconcerting. An upside-down head is weird enough, but a chuckling one is wayyyyyy out there. Then she said, "There is a place used often for rituals. It is an abandoned resort outside of town."

"Resort?" asked Olivia with surprise.

"Yes. It is owned by the Society of Jack-O'-Lanterns, known as the Society for short. Do you know of them?"

We all shook our heads like a bunch of retards in calculus class.

Morris said, "It is a very old Society, with roots stretching back to England prior to the founding of America. The way the basic Society operates today is to find women, and occasionally men, with great potential to either become very good members of Society or at least leaders, but they're in a terrible situation. Most of them are sex workers of some type, forced into that by circumstances — extreme abuse and trauma, such as incest, child pornography, captivity. The Society keeps them in that role for at least a year. They are live-in slaves at one of the houses, where they continue as sex workers. They're under contract. If they walk away, they walk away rich." She sighed. "Rarely do any walk away. Even those that walk away and don't continue, they're always part of the Society and doing things in business and other fields that come back to benefit the Society indirectly."

"Establishing freedom by slavery?" asked Olivia skeptically. Look, she's smarter than me. She could follow this bullshit.

"Something like that. The Society does a full psychological rebuild of the victim. This isn't casual, isn't play. They're dealing with victims with significant abuse, as I said — incest, gang-rapes, murder attempts, this sort of thing. They need the time and structure of the year in the house for the safety and isolation needed to basically rewire their brains."

Olivia frowned and her voice had a cold tone that told me she was pissed-off. "Trauma victims can be treated other, better ways."

Morris nodded, which was pretty fucking freaky looking. "Sure. But there's an additional factor. The Society's main leadership is an inner council of thirteen members, and they're supported by select, powerful members in the upper echelon. Only those in the very upper echelon of the Society know this hidden agenda. Ninety percent of the rank and file do not. The victims are those that are potentially channelers, based on DNA and background profiles."

Arching an eyebrow and folding her hands over her chest, Olivia said, "Okay, now I see where this crap is going."

"Yes. The manifestation rate is very low, not even one percent. Not even a tenth of a percent. The Consortium, a group of paranormals and others that has other objectives, has its hooks in the Society at the upper levels. It has done several other studies and other attempts at achieving this, but the Society works very well for them because, as I said, the process accomplishes multiple goals at once."

"Okay. So, the girls are slaves for a year," I said, still wrapping my head around this shit.

"Basically. They have Society dinners every couple of weeks, and they're placed into bondage and made to serve at the dinner to see if they score sex contacts. It's mostly to determine who is the most driven to succeed, useful in the channeling aspect, but also just for basic psychological information."

"This sounds like some sick medical experimentation bullshit hidden under porn," I muttered.

"Actually, it sounds like a cult," said Olivia with obvious anger.

"It is much more sophisticated. Regardless, the Society itself is not the problem. For perhaps eighty percent of the members, the Society functions as it should and, bizarre as it sounds, it does help people.

"The research is the problem, and that's where the resort comes in. The Society started this type of research in the 1960s and used the resort as one of several staging grounds. It is where I . . . not exactly died but, ah, wound up like this." She paused, clearly sad. "But that is the past. The Society used the resort as it is isolated and idea for paranormal experimentation. It has a lot of rooms, open areas for channeling, and they own most of the law officials in the county. But in '75, there was an incident . . . which was largely covered up by using one of their rising members to take the fall, explaining away a paranormal ritual murder as a DUI, and then everything shut down and they moved on to other places."[1]

---

[1] For readers of the Society series, this *is* related to Hunter Stone's DUI as shown in

"Nasty," said Olivia.

I was mostly keeping quiet. I was afraid if I talked, I'd barf. Besides, this was more her area. Throw my ass in a Chevron against a gunman and I'm your girl. This medical experimentation conspiracy shit threw me a bit.

"How do you know this?" asked Woody suspiciously. Or as suspiciously as a marionette can ask anything.

"My soul is attached to the area. I can be in places where I moved in life, or go somewhere if called, as I have done here. I see things."

"You see a guy named Flannagan?" asked Woody.

"No. He is unfamiliar."

"When will things happen?" I asked.

"Soon, likely tonight. Rituals always take place at night, trust me. There is risk to holding a captive. And they likely don't need to delay. They need power. If they have acted, as you have said, to clear out the warehouse, they are ready," she said with a little panic in her voice.

"How do we get there?" asked Olivia.

Morris gave directions. I gave Woody a look. He shrugged. It seemed a little weird to follow a ghost's instructions, but then again, to most people it seems a little weird to flush a guy's head in the toilet while you jerk him off and I've done that, so what the Hell.

Olivia nodded. "When we get there, will you manifest?"

"If I can. They work to screen out ghosts, but I am more powerful than the typical entity," she said.

"Then we'll see you there," said Olivia.

---

novel 3, <u>The Achilles Heel</u>

Chapter Eleven
Showdown

"Nice place if you want a fixer-upper," I muttered as we studied the long-abandoned resort east of town. Well, not exactly east of town. We were off the beaten path that leads to off the beaten path, if you know what I mean. I was now in Cube gear, while Olivia was in gray pants and a green shirt and jacket.

The property was sixty acres surrounded by a six-foot high stone wall that looked like something from one of those shows about castles and the middle ages. I expected King Arthur to come strolling out. Well, no. Because the actual resort was a piece of shit, at least on the outside.

The resort had three buildings. There was a central core that probably used to be administration, then two wings that jutted out at an angle like wings on an airplane. Each was five stories tall.

The buildings were constructed from this sort of wall composite that had rocks in it, and they were covered in rust and bird shit. The roof was a wreck, with actual holes. One wing had a tree growing out of the top. All around the property, the parking lot was ripped up and buried under dirt, weeds, and fallen trees.

This was what we made out on infare. After the ritual and cleaning up barf, Olivia and I raced into town and got some essential crime fighting gear. Woody knew how to use and program all of it.

God fucking knows how or when. It's best not to ask those questions of a pup- er, marionette.

Anyhow, Morris said the indoor swimming pool was under the administration building and was the most likely spot to be rehabbed and the location of the sacrifice. Which left a problem.

"Security is grade-A," said Woody.

Olivia bit her lip. We were parked across the road and down a half-a-mile. Aural detectors are things that allowed paranormals to sense other paranormal auras. They had lit up like fucking fourth of July when we got about a mile away. Normally, paranormals hide their auras, but these guys obviously figured no one in their right mind would be out here for any reason whatsoever, unless they were maybe hunting moose or coyotes or bears or mountain lions.

"I'm a city girl. We don't have this shit in Fullerton or in Vegas."

I'm not happy.

Olivia finally said, "We can't get in without getting spotted. No way. That's prime security."

Woody gave her a look, or at least as much as a marionette can do that. "Who taught you security?"

"I dated a guy who worked for a firm. That's a new gate despite this piece of shit place, and those poles along the top are new. They probably have electronic and heat-based surveillance and lasers to zap shit. The only way in is via the front door, and we don't have key. And given how remote this shithole is, the old 'my car broke down trick' is not likely to work."

Woody looked at me. "She's Miss Positive, ain't she?"

"Hey, she's right." I frowned. We were parked off the two-lane, piece of shit entry highway in a ditch and well hidden by shrubs and trees. The road was a lined but two-lane highway with no shoulder. No one was likely to see us, and if they did, the probably figured we ran off the road and hit a tree. So, I offered my thoughts on the subject. "Hey, Morris said whatever is gonna happen will happen tonight. Look, this screening gem I have protects us from electronic surveillance, it wipes us. So there's no risk to sitting here. We just rough it and wait for whoever is going to do whatever to show up."

The screening gem? Oh, I had picked it up a while back in a raid on a pawn shop selling totems. I realized what it was when the Cube never showed up on security footage, and then Olivia and I confirmed it. With the battle at Davis' warehouse, that meant the Cube had two major successes no one fucking new about. That sucks dirty ass, but those are the breaks of the game.

Oliva made a face. "Ugh. But you're right. Let's watch the place in shifts, agreed?"

"I'll handle it," said Woody. "I don't need sleep and mosquitos don't bother me."

"Well, I think we'll stay awake if we can," said Olivia. "The Cube here needs to post her social media."

I admit it, I blushed. Geez. "Sure, mom."

Olivia spanked her butt and said, "I'm so naughty."

We sat in the backseat and worked on using our phones to post. Woody kept an eye out. Given his size and coloring, it was easy for him to sit in a tree and watch everything. Even if spotted, someone would probably figure he was, like, an owl. Or a big crow.

We posted pretty well. Some comments annoyed me. Some people are utter douche bags and far too many people said my ass looked fat. That's just not true. And fortunately, we didn't have to wait long, because soon I was going to need to pee.

"Incoming," said Woody, landing with a thump on the hood and scrambling inside.

We ducked down in the car.

A car came along at a high rate of speed with only one working headlight. It was a decent car, other than the fucked-up headlight, probably some type of Toyota Supra.

It raced past, but quickly slowed and stopped at the gate.

We moved. Moving behind the scrubs and using the infrared, we could see easily, but no way could the driver spot us.

As we closed, I realized she looked . . . familiar.

Then I gasped. "Fuck. *Shauna*!"

Olivia looked at me. "You know her?"

"Yeah, I . . . man," I said, genuinely shocked.

Woody said, "You know her well?"

I shook my head. "No. I've worked with her on outcalls three times, but one of those times was just yesterday."

We were close to the car now. Shauna was wearing black booties, black pants, and a black rain jacket. It had started to rain lightly and was humid as fuck.

"Okay, listen up," said Woody, nodding at Shauna, who was using her phone to communicate via text, obvious with someone inside. "I'll hop on the bottom of the car ride in, plant a tracer on the car, and then open the gate for you two. On a night like this, she's sure to park right by the best way in."

I had no other plan, so I said, "Sure, go for it."

"Right," he said, and he was off.

I looked at Olivia and said, "I'm a little annoyed at this overgrown puppet taking charge."

She smiled. "At least he's not Kermit the Frog."

We watched as he quickly and surprisingly quietly raced across the road and rolled under the car. After two more minutes, Shauna moved to the black iron gate. There was a loud click and then she was able to manually roll it to the left. The rain was picking up, and we could see lightning in the distance.

"I hope that condo for termites hurries up. I don't really wanna sit out here in a thunderstorm," I said to Olivia, nodding at the sky. The lightning and thunder weren't far off.

"All I know is next time I want to add to my act, I'm buying a bird."

Shauna drove through, then got out and moved the gate.

"Why doesn't it have automated control?" I asked Olivia.

"I don't know. You're the superhero. You tell me," she said, watching Woody.

"You're the one who fucked a security guy."

Olivia smiled wickedly. "Hey, I was busy with his dick, not his profession."

I rolled my eyes. "We'll have this conversation when I'm not the Cube and you're not still dressed like someone who hit a Target sale."

She snorted.

The gate opened. Woody was able to roll it. It was big, but it was on a track, and he only had to move it a few feet. The rain was coming down fairly hard now. We raced over, brushing the hair out of our eyes., lightning displaying us in a sort of weird, strobe-light effect.

"Follow me," he said.

We did through what were once lovely flagstone sidewalks and flower gardens that were now barely visible through brush and trees. As we neared the right wing, we saw the car, parked by a side door at the end of the wing. We saw a light, undoubtedly Shauna using a flashlight. Then it vanished.

We reached the gray metal door, which was new and had a fresh lock.

I pushed. "locked. I'll blow it down."

Olivia grabbed my shoulder. "No, they'll hear. Locks are my thing."

She moved forward and used a magician's lockpick, which could probably be used to break into the room where the red button is at the White House. It was that effective. In four seconds, the door popped open.

We moved inside. Woody hissed at me, "You sure the screening gem still works?"

"If it doesn't, we'll find out in a hurry when they show up to kick our ass."

"Assuming there *are* more people," said Olivia. "Maybe Shauna is the only one here."

"I don't think so," said Woody. "She called someone from the gate, remember?"

"Good point," said Olivia with a sheepish look.

The hallway had emergency lighting, tiny bubbles in the floor, and they weren't battery operated, so there had to be some type of generator here because there's no way the place was getting power from town. Any town. The wallpaper had to be the same as in 1975 when the place shut down, a pattern of green flowers on white, the bottom half of the walls cheap wood paneling. The carpeting was long gone and all that was left was stained linoleum. The doors were like hotel doors — staggered, red, all shut.

"Place gives the hooker-me flashbacks," I muttered.

Suddenly, Morris appeared as a vision in front of us. I gasped.

"They are acting very soon. There's a door from what used to be the check-in desk that leads to the bleachers surrounding the old swimming pool. You must go there now," she said anxiously.

"How many are there?" asked Woody.

"Three."

I punched a hand into my fist. "Cube time, motherfuckers!"

Morris vanished, which was good. I still wanted to toss my cookies every time I saw her.

But I was gonna see much worse things before this was over.

"Jesus Christ," I whispered on seeing the set up below us.

"He ain't got nothing to do with this fuck-fest," said Woody.

We were at one of the four entryways to the pool area. The pool originally had been a triangle shaped pool with bleachers. Some of the bleachers were gone, so there were these random poles and twisted metal sticking around everywhere.

The pool itself was full of fluid, but it wasn't just water. There was an oval vat under the girl. Around the rest of the pool was water, which is normal. You need water for coolant for portals, sort of like cold water stops a hurricane. Sam explained this to me once. Anyhow, the vat was *not* water. It was sort of white and bubbling and boiling. There seemed to be vapor rising from it.

"What's that under her?" I asked.

"Hot wax," said Olivia grimly.

"Shit."

I studied the set up. "What are they doing? Is it geometry channeling?"

"Geometric," corrected Woody with obvious annoyance at my ignorance. Well, fuck him.

Geometric channeling was something neither Olivia nor I knew much about. We'd heard of it. Putting channelers or TMs in perfect shapes exponentially increased the power, which allowed users to do things like open portals or other shit.

The pool was an equilateral triangle, perfect for geometric channeling with a person at each point. But the horrifying aspect was that hovering over the triangle was a nude girl who looked sort of like the kind of blonde on blue girl used for college recruitment ads. She was a little chunky, but cute with freckles and straight blonde hair parted in the middle. She was also naked, covered in bruises and cuts, gagged, and bound in a horrible fashion. She was hung on a block and tackle upside down, her ankles bound to it. Her arms were pulled below her by a huge weight that hung just above the layer of wax, so her fingers were probably two feet above the threshold. She was soaked in sweat and blood, and clearly exhausted, her eyes shut but eyelids quivering.

As the Cube, you live to shut shit like this down.

Olivia nudged me. "Look. They're here."

At that moment, Shauna entered. With her were two more people I knew.

"Fuck my ass. The Rowes!" I hissed.

"Who?" asked Olivia.

"God damn," I muttered.

Now, I hated it when worlds collided. The world of Shelby the call girl should never interfere with the world of Shelby the Cube. It's like when a run into a guy I've fucked with his wife at the grocery store — believe it or not, this has happened three fucking times. Hey, cheaters eat, and so do hookers. Anyhow, I had this weird moment of nausea where I realized I had been eating these fucks just two days ago.

Then I was angry.

I started to move, but Woody and Olivia both grabbed one of my arms. Woody said, "Hold on, lead foot. We need a plan."

"The plan is we channel their asses into the vat, and they die," I snapped.

"They've got aural blockers around the pool," snapped Woody.

I paused. Aural blockers prevented channeling in an area. Us channelers could feel them sometimes. I didn't feel them.

Olivia looked at Woody. "Won't that negate their work?"

He put up a finger and said, "I reached out carefully. They've got a band, like a ring around the pool area. Won't affect them and actually won't stop us out here. But we can't get channeling *through* the band. We've got to get inside the triangle and attack from there."

"Shit," I said, unable to think of a snappy comeback. This news royally sucked.

Olivia smiled. "There's actually a very easy way to do that, BFF."

"Oh?"

She pointed. "We rush them like frat members at a sorority initiation party."

"Shit, good thinking."

"But we have to split up," said Woody. "We've got to take them all at once. Once we attack, they can use channeling, TM, inside the triangle as well."

"Can't we just throw something at them?" I asked.

"There's nothing around other than some bleacher parts," said Olivia. "And if we use wind or earth, they can counter that. They think they're alone. They'll *never* expect a physical attack."

"You're right, kid, but there's a problem with that," said Woody, rubbing his chin. Well, what passes for a chin on a marionette. "The chick over the vat. They could just drop her. If each one of us is tied up fighting, then no one is left to rescue her."

"I can handle that. I know Shauna, and I know her idea of a good workout is eating standing up instead of sitting down," I said confidently.

Woody looked at me, saw the confidence in my eyes, and said, "Okay, Cube." He turned to Olivia. "You've got long legs. Big daddy is on the other side of the pool. You run over there, and when we get into position, use your text to set a five count. I'll take the Rowe broad. We go on zero."

"Right," said Olivia.

She kissed me, said, "I love you," then she was off. I didn't even get a chance to respond. She was wound the fuck up.

I looked at Woody. "Well, woodlice, I hope this works."

"If it don't, it's your fault, kid, it's your plan. I'm moving."

"Thanks for the pep-talk, termite head."

We split up. There were gaps under the remaining bleachers that made it very easy to get with just a few feet of the TMs. There were corridors in the bleachers. Sneaking up on them was easy. They were extremely focused on their task at hand, which was complicated and would boil their skin if they fucked it up, so they couldn't have mistakes. Hey, were convinced they were alone and in the efficiency of their detectors and aural blocker ring, both of which we were gonna beat. And enough of the bleachers were left to provide plenty of cover.

I knew where to look for Olivia and could see her. Shauna couldn't because she was standing and by the pool while I was crouching and under the darkness of the bleachers, right next to the corridor. The only flaw in our plan was we each had a slightly different distance to cover. But we figured surprise would negate that problem.

I got the silent text.

5

4

4

2

1

Zero

Go!!!!!!!!!!!!!!!!

What I did next makes me damn proud. I dove at Shauna's legs and hit the back of them. They had no clue an attack was coming. This pitched her forward, but I held her legs and pulled back, so she didn't fall into the pool. Instead, she crashed down and cracked her jaw on the end of the pool.

Even before she hit, I was moving. I channeled all the water in the pool into the vat. This did two things. First, it dispersed the psychic heat released when the spell broke up. Luckily, they had barely started, or we would have fried all our asses. Second, it cooled out the hot wax under block-and-tackle girl, so even if she fell, she wouldn't be burned alive. Which is always a good thing. And I kept the water level low enough so the Rowes wouldn't drown. Hey, I'm pretty good at this shit, no matter what the internet says.

Olivia took out Tony Rowe without any problem. She just ran at him and jumped, kicking him in the back and knocking him into the pool. When I channeled up, the wave carried him and landed his ass in the previously hot wax vat. The impact knocked him cold. At least he didn't lose a bunch of teeth like Shauna did.

Now, Michelle was just a tad more wary. She saw Olivia running at Tony, but that split-second didn't help. She turned to fight a human foe and instead saw Woody sliding across the floor. He'd run and then slid on his ass and hit her feet. He grabbed her and flipped her backwards into the pool. And like Tony, she was caught in my wave and slammed into the vat.

I got up and couldn't believe it was over so fast. The entire battle couldn't have taken more than two, three seconds.

Woody snapped me out of it. "We gotta secure them, Cube."

"You two do that. I'll help the girl," I said in my proud superheroine voice. I quickly checked Shauna. "She's out cold. She's lost a bunch of teeth, and I think her jaw is broken. She probably could use a doctor."

"When we're done," said Woody. "They're dangerous if they wake up."

"Sure."

By standing on the edge of the vat, I still couldn't reach the girl intended for sacrifice. She could see me and the look of relief on her face was enormous. Olivia got into the vat and began tying up the Rowes with some extension cords she found in a supply closet. Obviously, the place had lights and was run off a generator, so there were tons of cords. It was kind of funny. They looked kind of cute tied up in multi-colored cords.

I moved to the side wall and manually shifted the block and tackle, lowering the girl to the base of the vat. Olivia and Woody got the Rowes out of the vat.

Once the girl was down, Olivia helped slowly guide her, so she was on her right side, then Olivia started untying her hands. They were purple.

I quickly raced to them and said, "I'm the Cube. You're okay."

Once I removed her gag, she started to cry.

"Honey, it's okay. What's your name?"

"C-c-carol."

"Well, I'm glad to meet you. And don't worry. You're safe. No one will ever hurt you again."

She was free now and hugged me like a child hugging her mother. Knowing she was safe was one of the best damn moments of my life.

Some days . . . it's fun being a superheroine.

Chapter Twelve
Visiting Friends and Enemies . . . and Sometimes Both

So . . . three days later, Monday the fifth, once Carol was home from the hospital . . . the Cube made a visit. I had to talk to Carol. She was our only lead. Based on Carol's accusations and some compelling evidence because the dumb fucks recorded their torture of her, Shauna and the Rowes were in maximum security. No way could we interrogate them, at least until Medina got them transferred to Ops prison, if that was even possible. Carol was our last hope of getting to the source of the cult quickly.

Olivia tried to call up Morris over the weekend, but nothing happened. We took that to assume putting down the cult at the resort enabled her to move on. Well, that's what I hope. She made me vomit, but she helped a lot and was pretty nice. Besides, no one should be stuck in limbo forever.

Anyhow, having a chat with Carol wasn't as easy as you might think. She had a shitload of people around her house, which was a permanently anchored mobile home in that park in Henderson off the 515, you know the one. It was pretty. Green with lots of hanging plants and a nice artificial turf yard around it, even a white picket fence and a bar-b-que.

Her mom was around all the time, as one might expect for a single parent who had her teenage daughter sucked in by a cult and nearly dropped in a vat of hot wax. I wasn't worried about her mom. Her name was Patty, and she was a really fat woman with curly black hair, glasses, and a perpetually bemused look. One of those life-long secretary types.

Being the middle of the night, the press was no longer an issue either.

But the place was also being staked out by the WSA — the World Security Agency, you know, the global parallel to the NSA. There were two of them parked in a black Honda Accord across the street. Being the Cube, I'm well versed in surveillance and spotted them instantly.

I left them to Olivia.

At 2:12 on Monday morning (or Sunday night, it's your preference), they were sitting pretending to look at a map. They were parked in the lot of a former K-Mart that was now a Dollar store or some shit like that. Anyhow, it was hot even in the middle of the night. They had to be baking. You'd think they could afford a better gig.

I learned later their names were Sam and Steve, a black guy with a square head and a white guy blond on blue with a square head. Frankly, in this neighborhood, their good looks, physique, and nice car made them ultra-conspicuous. But the WSA always liked to hang out in style, or so I've been told by others.

Anyhow, I was waiting by the entrance to the trailer park. A minute later, Olivia comes along. She's dressed in ultra-slut makeup and is wearing a white bodice that has half the loops missed. She's basically flashing nipple with every move. Jeans shorts and ripped nylons with black booties finish off the outfit.

She saunters right up to the driver's side where Steve is clearly appalled. And she says in a blurry tone, "Hey, you're cute. Wanna fuck, baby?"

Sam is looking around, suspicious. But not for the right things.

"Sorry, lady, we're gay," said Steve.

Olivia made a face, then took a compact out of her black purse. She blew on it.

Lights out.

The compact was really a totem that, combined with a little necromantic sleeping powder, gave them the sleep of Rumpelstiltskin. Out cold.

In my Kevlar mesh as the Cube, I slipped inside the property of the trailer park. Picking locks was easy. Hey, Olivia was a magician. The first thing she taught me was lockpicks. Anyhow, they had electronic security, but I wasn't worried. I was in Cube Kevlar.

Once at the trailer, I knocked on the door and said, "Miss Austin, it's the Cube, Carol's friend."

Patty opened the door with shock on her face.

"It's you! You *came*," she said with a hoarse whisper and obvious surprise.

"Of course. Where is Carol? I have limited time, I'm sorry," I said.

"Oh, sure. Carol is in her room."

The trailer was nice but low-rent. Picture the trailer in *Rockford Files* but with an aquarium.

Once I reached Carol in the back bedroom, I saw her eyes widen with happy shock. "The Cube! Wow! You really came!"

"Hey, you're my friend," I said, hugging her. "I'm always glad to help. Not to be rude, but my time is limited. My partner is distracting the douche bags across the street."

Carol laughed. "They're so out of place."

"I know," I said with a smile.

She looked at me. "You said, like, I could talk any time I needed to, right? Right?"

"Sure."

"The cult . . . I . . . when I was in the hospital, there was one thing I didn't tell the police. I . . . I was scared. Scared they'd lock me up. But they . . . they have a leader who . . . they'll kill me." She shut her eyes and rocked on the bed out of fear.

"No, they won't. I'm here now, part of your life, part of your family," I said, reassuring her with a firm hold on her shoulder.

She nodded, took out her phone, and pulled up a picture. She held up the phone for me and said, "He's the leader. I swear on my mother's life."

I looked at the photo.

And at that moment, life became motherfucking complicated . . . in the extreme.

I looked at her. "I believe you."

"You *do*?" she asked, stunned.

"I do. And I will stop him, but it will take a few days to make a plan. You're safe here. I have a partner, chick with brown hair, looks like a dancer on the Strip. Don't let appearances fool you. She's sharp. Nothing will happen."

"You sure?"

"I'm sure." I smiled. "You're my friend. I don't let my friends down."

"I . . . thank you."

I looked at Patty, then at Carol. "I must go. I'm really sorry. Your email will be monitored, but I'll set up a private account where we can talk. I'll mail you a letter tomorrow."

"Okay, that's cool," said Carole.

I kissed her cheek. "It will get better."

Patty helped me to the door and said, "Thank you so much. Will she really get better?"

'Yep. I'll make sure of it."

I left and met Olivia sitting on the hood of the WSA car, her right boob completely showing. She smiled and said, "One look at my knockout tits and they passed out."

I laughed. "Yeah, I'm not buying that one."

She put on a mock pout and fastened the bodice enough to keep her boobs in, then asked, "You get what you need?"

"Yeahhhhhhhhhhh . . . let's get out of here before we talk."

Surprised, she made a face. We got back to her Stinger and raced back into Vegas. After a minute, she asked, "What's got your panties in a bunch?"

"She IDed the leader of the cult," I said glumly. I was still wearing my mask, even though the Stinger had tinted windows.

"Well? Who is he?"

"I . . . let's get back to your place. I want Woody to hear, and we're going to have to talk to Medina."

"God damn, that's annoying! Fine, I'll have us home in nine minutes, tops."

She was true to her word, breaking several traffic laws in the process. By the time we got to the condo, I had ditched the mask and covered the Kevlar with a red hoodie with yellow stars and a pair of baggy jeans. We entered the condo to find Woody sitting on the sofa watching talking heads yap about some earthquake some place I had never heard of.

"Hey, you're back! You get the goods?" he asked, jumping up like a housewife eager to see her man home from work.

"Sort of. I know who hooked *her* in. Let's talk. But we're gonna have to talk to Medina about all of this."

I got a beer. Olivia grabbed a water. We sat at the table, which was covered in unopened packages of cat food from Amazon (Fancy Feast, little fuckers won't eat anything else). Olivia and I had put our purses on the table as well.

"Lemme get outta this shit," I said, referring to my Cube clothes.

"Go for it."

Olivia and Woody talked about the news as I quickly changed. I returned in a minute wearing dark green leggings, a yellow camisole, and bunny slippers. Then I sat at the table, took a swig of beer, and said, "I know the man she identified. Bob Toberman."

"That's kind of a downer after I broke all the laws of the road to get us home an hear this name. Who is *he*?" asked Olivia.

I sighed. "He's a guy who was on the Empire's list. I never fucked him. But we all heard about him. He's one of those guys that fulfills the old stereotype of one bad apple in every bush, or as I prefer to say, one floating turd in a toilet. He had a girl on a call and nearly beat her to death with a golf club because she agreed to backdoor action but then wanted him to stop because of, uh, fit issues."

"Oh," aid Olivia, looking a little surprised and worried.

"But he's also the main coke mover in this town and is known for liking little girls."

Woody said, "How little?"

"He likes girls, not children. Picture me as a hot fifteen-year-old and you have his preferred client."

"Hard to do as old as you are," said Woody with a grin.

I slapped his face and said, "I can still feed you to the termites!"

"I'm shellacked."

I rolled my eyes.

"Okay, so he would seem to be the top man. Is he paranormal?" asked Olivia.

"Unlikely. This is why we should talk to Medina. But from what I see, he's gotta running totems with drugs. That makes all of this fit. Hookers make good runners, so it's easy to see Shauna getting involved. She was a single mom. Desperate and not too bright, the perfect sucker."

"How do we take him down? Walk onto his favorite golf course and return the club-pounding favor?" asked Olivia.

I shook my head. "No way. If he's into totems, even if he's not paranormal, he must have an idea of their power. He could have some totem that turns me inside out or turns me into a dog or some shit."

"Yeahhhhhhhh . . . we gotta be cagey about this," said Woody. "We don't need you pissing on the carpet once you're a dog."

I gave him the one-finger salute.

Olivia rose and got a beer. "You've driven me to drinking."

Woody suddenly said, "So we broke up whatever distribution Davis and the Rowes were doing. But we don't know how much that hurts the cult or him because we don't know if he's in this for the money or running some type of paranormal plan or needed those totems for his cult. And since Medina told us Davis had a heart attack in the hospital and is probably not going to wake up, we're not likely to find out from him."

"Pretty much summed it up," I said. Olivia handed me a second beer. I took a big swig, then said, "We could just forget about it. But I'm worried one day he'll figure out it was us and come after us, and I'm worried he'll come after Carol. We can't spend the rest of our lives babysitting her, no matter what I told her mom. Besides," and I pointed at Woody, "since this idiot is part of the Cube's entourage now, I owe it to him to blow up the cult and help him find his sister."

"Thanks, kid," he said.

Olivia nodded. "Well, okay, on a practical level, how would we get to him, anyhow?"

I laughed. "Oh, that we can manage."

I said nothing. Olivia finally said, "Well?"

"Wait for it. This is my dramatic moment, baby," I said with a smile.

She gave me the finger.

Finally, I said, "I just have to become a coke whore."

"Barry! It's been almost two months, fuck-face. You find another whore?" I joked, hugging him as I stepped into the doorway of his home on the outskirts of Henderson on Monday evening around dusk.

I was fucking tired. I'd been up all night with Carol, then had kickboxing, then was on call 12-6 and had two backdoor sessions. But time was valuable. We'd already lost three days since saving Carol at the resort.

"No way, tight-ass," said Barry with a wink. "I've just been busier than Hell. God damn, you look good enough to eat."

I smiled. I knew that was true. I was wearing black boots with laces up the middle that went thigh-high, a black leather skirt, and a white bodice. It was utter slut. Being a hooker means actually dressing differently for every job. Barry had clients at his house, so there was no pretense, and he liked the slutty look. "Thanks. You're looking good, too."

He winked. "Been doing cardio. C'mon, let's go out to the pool."

Barry Davidson, you may recall if you're fucking paying attention and not jacking off while you read my book, is one of my regulars who is also a cocaine cowboy. He was going to be my route to Toberman.

I hoped.

We walked to his pool, which admittedly was pretty damn nice. The pool was huge and shaped like a triangle. There was a diving board with the deep end was a full fifteen feet deep. Around the pool was a three-foot tall fence that was built with cement Roman columns, and the entry from the house was also in Roman style. Around the pool deck were several tables and chairs, all with umbrellas to keep out the hot Vegas sun.

As we pass into the pool deck, I raise my hands and a large Samoan man wearing a blue suit moves towards me. Like I said, Barry's been my regular for a time now, and there's one standard rule. Strip-search. Not unusual for these cocaine movers. To say they're paranoid is just not even getting to the meaning of the word.

"Hey, Junior, you've lost weight," I joked, and began taking off my skirt.

He smiled. He had short, black hair, sunglasses, the suit, and had to be 350. Saying he lost weight is like saying a mountain lost a rock.

I stripped quickly, except for the boots. I had to sit in a chair an unlace them halfway to get them to slide off. As I did this, I bitched, "These fucking boots cost $2,600 and they aren't worth shit."

"Boots are a rip-off," said Barry, sitting at a table on the other side of the door, getting out his blow.

Yellowjackets buzzed us. It was a nice night, about eighty, warm dry desert air blowing. Once I got the boots off, he ran a something over my clothes. Meanwhile, I stood up and assumed the position, planting my hands on the table. I was fully shaved and clean.

As Junior put on gloves, I looked back and said sexily, "Be gentle, baby, it's my first time."

Junior was one of those big, silent types, but he did crack a smile. Then I grimaced as he checked out both holes. They weren't after weapons. They were after wires. And it didn't matter that I had been here at least half a dozen times. In fact, in some ways, that made them more paranoid.

I don't know how people live like this. No wonder they eventually go nuts and wind up shooting each other, unless they get tossed in the slammer first. I bet I could make a fortune selling these guys off-market Xanax.

Anyhow, Junior checks me out good. I learned after the first couple cavity searches its best to relax. Getting tight just makes it hurt more. Junior has a little habit of touching my clit while he's doing it, which of course is not technically the process, but it gets him off. Once Junior is done, he turns to Barry and said, "All clear."

I smile and say, "Of course."

Barry smiled. "That got me a little excited."

"Me, too," I lied. "Can I put my boots back on? It might turn you on and, well, they cost a lot. I don't want them just lying around."

"Sure, baby."

I make a show of slowly putting them on and lacing them up, and he's getting as hard as a California redwood. Or one of those big fucking trees, whatever they're called. Anyhow, once I get the boots on, I approach and tell him, "You've missed me."

"Ah, you're right there."

I unzip his pants and take out his member and get to work with a blow job, which after all is what I'm paid for. This is a weird appointment, though. The worlds of Shelby the call girl and Shelby the Cube should never meet, but now they do. I gotta be Shelby the hooker to get to Toberman, but only the Cube wants to get to Toberman.

This makes it difficult. Olivia talks about compartmentalization, how part of the brain does one thing and the other side another. Sometimes it's good, allows people to focus in emergencies. Sometimes it's bad, like when a Nazi guard would gas people and walk next door into the house and listen to music and have dinner with the family.

Being a hooker is about pleasing the other person, but I'm really anxious and that's throwing me off. The only thing that saves me is Barry is into his coke as much as me, and I could have been some street walking crack-whore in Hollywood Hills, and he'd *still* have loved my blow job.

I'm working on him for several minutes. Now, giving a blow job can be a lot of fun or very tedious. This one is tedious, because I'm not here on the job, not in my head. I'm here to kick Toberman's ass. So, this is just a means to an end, and as a result, I'm off my call girl game. My jaw starts to hurt, and I start doing more jacking off than using the mouth to try and get him off before the coke really sets in and stops him from coming. Blow jobs are really more suck-hand jobs than just sucking a cock. That's certainly true of guys on coke. They need the added stimulation.

Finally, I get him to the big moment. I can feel that push that's the precursor of the final shot. I really ramp up and start moaning and groaning the way guys like. Why they like this, I don't know. It's the way they're built.

Then he shoots in my mouth. I'm quite willing to eat cum, unlike a lot of girls, which I learned early on helps with tips and with referrals. Guys always go back to a girl who swallows. It's not like I really like the stuff. Well, I do. There's a certain sense of pride in seeing them explode. And most of the time, it tastes okay, like wet pretzels. Some girls hate the taste. Anyhow, I swallow him down. Then I slowly stand up, lick my lips, and tell him, "That was really good, baby. We're gonna have fun tonight."

"You bet. Hey, if you can get Toberman these girls, you're doing me a huge favor, baby. This isn't bullshit, is it?"

"No way. They're my cousins, and they're sluts. I told you, I can't get them legit hooker jobs because they're fifteen and sixteen. But they want in on the action."

He nodded and snorted some more coke.

I felt someone move behind me and turned to see Junior, who had pulled down his pants and was stroking a short but fat member. I smiled and said, "Hey, baby, you need some help?"

"I surely do."

I went down on him, getting on my knees on the pool deck before him. That wasn't all that comfortable, but I knew he wouldn't last long. Junior was always a freebee when doing Barry. It was just part of the package, like the strip-search. Hey, Barry usually paid me several thousand dollars and never haggled. That's worth a lot.

Junior groaned and got near his point. I knew what he liked. I pulled my mouth off him and stroked him to climax, spraying his seed in my hair and on my face. Then I wiped off my face with my hand and licked it up. "Good meal. Thanks, baby."

"Welcome."

He helped me to my feet as Barry said, "The big guy wants to see you in the den and close this out."

"Sure," I said. I made sure I didn't have cum dripping on my face before getting dressed. Not much I could do about my hair. Not the ideal appearance for a meeting, but hey, he knew I was a call girl.

Barry led me to a den, which was really a fancy office with a lot of expensive, strange looking, black volcanic glass furniture. The place was immaculate. I couldn't imagine how he kept it clean, given the desk was all glass and most of the dressers and cabinets were the same. Well, you know, the poor are crazy and the rich eccentric.

The room was about eight-hundred square feet, the desk back against a window overlooking the pool. The glass was one-way, which I knew because I hadn't been able to see inside when out on the pool.

I've told you about my categorization for people, right? Toberman immediately went into the power-tripper slot. He had a mostly bald head, with a little short, black hair on the back. His eyes were dark and cold, the sort of eyes that could stick a knife in a kitten and smile. His face was handsome, but in an angry, violent way, with a jutting chin. In terms of figure, he was at least fifty, but he looked thirty-five, and was in surprisingly great shape. I wondered about steroids. All of his movements were aggressive. He was clearly in command of any room he was in. I knew immediately I had to play this cautiously and submissively.

"This is the broad, boss. Shelby."

"Good to meet you, sir," I said, extending my hand.

He rose and looked me over like meat. Hey, I'm used to that. But with him it was more . . . personal. And I could pick up some heavy-duty aural blockers at work. I really hoped mine were working.

As he shook my hand, while still looking at me, he said to Barry, "Barry, the word broad went out of style when I was a kid. This is a lady. You can call me Toberman."

"Shelby. Thank you, sir. I understand from Barry you have certain . . . interests. I have interests, too. My interest is cold, hard cash. Yours is this."

I slowly reached into my purse and pulled out an old pic of Olivia when she was sixteen. She looked innocent and demure. It was a Christmas photo. I handed it to him.

"She is worth my time," he said after a moment. "Who is she?"

"My cousin. I have two more, all fifteen or sixteen. They're into older guys. I can't get them legit hooking gigs because of their age, but they've been fucking since they were twelve. They'll keep their mouths shut."

He nodded. "I'll give you twenty grand per visit."

I nodded. "That works for me. All cash."

"All cash. You're part of my organization now, so I need to know where you are at all times."

I wasn't keen on that. I got a lot less keen on it when I found out what he really meant. "You want me on Life 360?"

"No. Barry, get her in position on the couch."

"Over here, blondie," he said.

I frowned. I wasn't sure what this as about, but I didn't like it. I liked it a lot fucking less when Barry said, "Lay down and pull your legs up to your chest."

I played it off and said, "Oooooh, baby wants a freebee?"

But then I saw Junior putting on a glove and some lube. I'm laying on my back with my knees up to give them a big, wide few of the happy parts and, even for someone of my profession, this was a little embarrassing. They were all dressed. I was buck naked.

Junior approached with something that was the size of a pencil eraser, but it had two little points on it.

"Uh, where is *that* going?" I asked with obvious alarm, because I *was* fucking alarmed.

"It's a tracer," snapped Toberman, walking over. "It pinches a little, like getting an IUD. Then we'll be on good terms because I'll know where you are."

"What is this about? Why are you doing this?"

"I know where my employees are at all times," he said with a glare. "Now, you going to go along, or do we tie you down and do it the old-school way with forceps?"

"I'm with you," I said hurriedly.

Junior looked less than thrilled as he inserted the device in me. It went in an unpleasant place. You figure it out.

"Ouch!" I snapped as it pinched. It hurt at first, but quickly faded away. Still, it was an unpleasant experience, to say the least.

Humiliated and angry, I sat up and put on my panties and skirt as I asked, "When do we first meet? I *want* my *cash*."

"Saturday."

"Why so long?"

"I have business to attend to Thursday and Friday."

I tried not to show how upset I was at being violated, so I rose and swung my cum-stained hair and said sassily, "I'm pretty smart. Can I help?"

He slapped me. It wasn't a hard slap, but it surprised the shit out of me. He snapped, "Mind your own business."

"Yes, sir," I said. "Is that it?"

"That's it."

"Oh," I said, definitely surprised he didn't want to take a run at me. I guess I was too old. Or maybe he didn't want sloppy seconds after his men . . . or he just had something against hookers. Some guys were like that. Anyhow, that was that.

Barry led me towards the car. I was ready. Toberman had a classic, black '78 Cadillac that he drove everywhere. It was in immaculate condition, spotless, just like his den. As we walked by, I paused and whistled. "Nice car."

"Yeah, it's his baby."

I pretended to examine it and slipped a tracer I had gotten from an online military supplier onto the bumper. The fucking thing cost me a week's pay, but it was worth it. It was military grade. It wasn't affected by anything and just looked like part of the license plate holder. Like all vain criminals, he had custom plates. His read, "CAD KING," which fit in more ways than one.

Barry took me back to my car and said, "Nice doing business with you. I hope your cousins like plenty of action. Toberman is like a total stud."

"They can take it," I said with a wink, starting the car and exiting.

As soon as I was a few blocks away and certain I wasn't being tailed, I tested my tracer. Perfect signal. Unfortunately, I was pretty sure the one inside me was doing the same thing.

I was wayyyyyyyy to pumped with adrenaline to feel any pain. Yet. Tomorrow, I'd be sore as fuck down there. And pissed.

I called Olivia. "I planted it on his pet Cadillac."

"Perfect."

"He liked your picture, baby," I said in a sexy voice. "I hope you like older men."

She laughed and matched my coy sexiness. "I like what you like, baby." Then seriously she said, "You read him?"

"Major league aural blockers. I don't know what he is, but it's not friendly."

"Well, we'll be ready for him."

"I hope so."

"Any problems?"

I hesitated, then said, "Yeah, well, one. A bit. He stuck a tracer up my hoo-hah. Hurt like a bitch."

"Baby! You okay?"

'Yeah, I will be. Like getting an IUD."

"I'll take care of you."

"I don't need that. I do have to stay at your place. I don't want him tracing me back to my place, if he decides to check me out."

"Sure. I need a maid," she said with a laugh.

"And I need you to take care of him."

Olivia said coldly, "Oh, we will, baby. His days as a member of the living are coming to a close."

Chapter Thirteen
Bad Night at Black Rock

Based on Barry's tip, Olivia, Woody, and I were ready to move on Thursday night, the eighth. We were assuming Toberman's reference to business was really a coke or totem deal. Using Olivia's Stinger as our undercover car wasn't exactly idea, but this is Vegas, after all, and full of snazzy and mid-life crisis cars.

The advantage we had was my tracer. Toberman was on the move around midnight after a really late and really long dinner at some fancy steakhouse. But oddly, he was going to the business district, not his home or the Strip. Granted, Vegas is a lady of the night, but even so, standard business still generally followed standard business hours. Certainly, there wasn't any normal business transacted at eleven at night, even in Vegas. That was the time for people like me and the strippers to be working. And the time for the movers of illicit trade to be moving.

Olivia wore a black hoodie and black pants with black mascara to muss up her face. She looked like someone who tried to dress up like Batgirl while she was drunk and failed miserably. I wore my Cube Kevlar. Woody was hiding in the trunk, but wired in via our coms, and he wore a British schoolboy black jacket with red trim. He looked like an idiot, even for a puppet. Marionette.

Keeping pace but keeping back, Olivia and I navigated traffic, which even in Vegas was starting to slow down this time of night once we were away from the Strip.

"Don't get too close," I warned.

"I got it. But where's he going? This isn't the warehouse district," she said, biting her lip.

"Just don't lose him."

She didn't. Having a friend as accomplished as Olivia is the luckiest break of my life. God doesn't really do much for you. It's your friends that count. I guess what matters is God gives you good friends.

However, I felt sick to my stomach when Toberman's driver, who was hauling his ass around in his fancy Cadillac, parked at a building I knew *very* well.

"Go past. Park at that garage around the corner," I snapped, pointing.

Olivia said nothing and did as I said. As he moved past the building, I stared at it.

The building was the home of Black Rock Insurance.

Once we parked, I looked at Olivia with alarm. "This is the home of Black Rock. This is where Barry works. This is where I fucked their CEO, Howard Cochran, a few days ago."

"This has to be a run, then. He's not here to buy life insurance," said Olivia sarcastically.

I hit the dashboard. "Damn. How do I get in there?"

Before Olivia could answer, Woody said, "Check the camera. It's picking up someone parking next to Toberman."

We watched and waited. The tires I didn't recognize. But the God damn fucking shoes I did. They were worn brown penny loafers that I had seen very recently.

God damn fuckwad Barry.

I balled my fist and got ready to curse, but before I could, we saw another set of legs. They were nude female, a girl, probably a teenager, with black heels.

I looked at Olivia with outrage, and she looked at me with worry. Finally, Woody said, "I'd ambush them now."

I moved to get out of the car, because I could walk to the building's underground lot easier than Olivia driving back around the block, but she put a hand on my arm. "No. Look, they're going inside."

I paused. Thank God Olivia was there, because my initial reaction was one of instinct and anger. But when she made me pause, I stopped to think and realized something. "This is a terrible place to trade underage girls. Something else is going on. Can you change the angle on my bug?"

Olivia nodded and we could see them walking to the elevator, which luckily for us was in front of the car. They keyed a code in. The girl was sort of like a young, Fullerton me — stringy blonde hair, freckles, green eyes, terrified. Her hands were tied behind her back. She wore black leggings and a red hoodie. But she wasn't gagged and wasn't screaming. She just looked defeated.

But I watched, because on the outside I could see the floors light up and knew where they were going.

"Fuck me with a broom."

"What?" asked Olivia with alarm.

"They're going to the penthouse. That's the office of Howard Cochran, the CEO. They're going right to the top, literally."

"Is he involved?" asked Olivia with surprise.

"Geez, boss, get a clue. Of course, he is," said Woody.

I nodded. "Termite-head is right. I mean, we know he spends his day fucking call girls since I was here just a few days ago. But this can't be just about girls and totems. I still don't know why they're meeting *here*."

"Does it matter?" asked Olivia.

I bit my lip. I wasn't sure.

Woody answered. "Yeah, it does. The cult has deep roots. Maybe this goes further."

I suddenly snapped, "It doesn't matter. I'm not letting a teenage girl get tortured or raped so we can get information. I'm going in."

"*We're* going in," said Olivia.

I nodded. I had no choice. She was the fucking magician, which made her a locksmith supreme. I sure as fuck wasn't getting inside without her.

Olivia said, "Don't they have security?"

"Not now," I said quickly. "First rule of conspiracy meetings, don't let them get taped. They'll have all the exterior security up now, but nothing inside this place will be on. They can't risk exposing themselves. And they don't need to, 'cause they figure they're alone. And I have the screening gem to protect us."

"How do we play this?" she asked, breathing hard. Olivia wasn't a fighter. She was an entertainer, a good one. Her ability to use necromancy was critical here.

"We need to locate them all — other than Toberman's driver. Looks like he's settled in to play on his phone in the driver's seat."

Woody said, "He'll stay put. He's got to be ready in case they need a fast exit."

"Olivia," I said, and I saw her shaking, "first thing, love, calm down."

"I'm calm, I'm calm," she said, as if she'd just taken a caffeine injection.

"No, you're not. Be calm."

"I will be. I'm fine."

I doubted that, but there was no time to prep her. "I sense their auras. Cochran and Toberman are going to the penthouse. Barry is in a room and the girl next to it. I'm guessing he tied her up somewhere and is nearby standing guard. Barry's a douche. Olivia, you take his ass down and rescue her."

"Right."

"I'll go up top and deal with our conspiracy players. This is a commercial building, so it's going to have all sorts of access in the suspended ceiling.

"My God, what kind of life is this where you know that?" asked Olivia.

"A fuckin' weird one. Olivia, when you finish, you back me up."

"What about me?" asked Woody.

"We can get to the stairs without the driver seeing us. They're over there," I said pointing behind the car. "But we need his ass taken out anyhow, so that's your job."

"Got it."

"Let's move." I kissed Olivia. She was too nervous to kiss back. Geez, Batman never had these problems.

We moved quickly and quietly. I had no desire to use the elevator. It made us a sitting target and might alert those inside someone was here.

We split up on the tenth floor. I patted Olivia's ass and said, "Kick ass, baby."

"Yep. You, too. Love you."

I went up the stairs, taking two at a time. Now, I'm sure some of you lard-asses work out in between reading shit like this book. If you want a real workout, take sixteen flights of stairs two at a time.

Once I got to the sixteenth floor, I immediately recognized the layout from my, uh, previous engagement. I found the stairs to the roof. They didn't have an alarm. I guessed Cochran sometimes liked to go the roof and enjoy the view. He was the type who probably came up here and jacked off thinking he was lord and master of Vegas. Douche.

On the roof, I found maintenance access to the penthouse. I was in luck. Cochran had custom designed it, and the maintenance workers, probably expecting more modifications, had made it very easy to get into the suspended ceiling and the cuts. Once inside, I easily took a screwdriver I kept in the Kevlar and undid one of the vents leading to the duct over the middle of the room. Those ducts are the cheapest shit on the planet.

Watching from above, I had a pretty good view. I was slightly behind Cochran, who was behind his desk. He wore a blue dress shirt and black pants with dress shoes. I'm guessing, but I don't think he'd been home since the work day ended. The desk was covered in papers and files. I started taking pictures.

In front of the desk was Toberman. He wore a black suit and looked like a mortician. If he chose to find out where I was at the moment, he'd shit his pants, but he had no reason to do that. He was clearly here on business, his jaw set.

The wee talking about wine, then Cochran sat. Toberman sat in front of him. With my restricted view, this is about all I could see, tough I could see Cochran's phone on the desk. They were alone, which made sense. They would want Barry downstairs guarding the girl.

"This should finish the deal," said Cochran, sliding a contract across the desk for Toberman.

"Excellent. I look forward to having a new yacht."

He signed some papers. I hoped my fucking phone was worth the money I had spent on upgrades and was getting all of this. God damn fucking Verizon.

Toberman slid the papers back and said, "I appreciate our efforts. I've wired two-fifty to your offshore accounts."

"Appreciated," said Cochran. He slid the papers into a locked drawer in his desk, clapped his hands, and said, "Now it's time to celebrate. It's not often one makes a quarter of a million dollars in six seconds."

Toberman chuckled.

Cochran reached into his desk and pulled out his gun.

"Olivia, Cochran has a .357," I hissed, though I wasn't positive it was a .357. Admittedly, I'm not an expert on guns. But I have learned a lot. Kevlar isn't like Iron Man's fucking armor, it has weaknesses at certain cartridge levels, so I've had to learn. Hey, I've learned about eating ass, too. I'm a multi-talented girl.

"I've got eyes on Barry and the girl. We're two floors down. No guards."

"We've gotta move."

"I agree. On three."

At the end of the countdown, I started to channel through the grate. I channeled hard and fast, you know, like a young man fucking.

Toberman looked surprised, which was nice to see.

Cochran yelped and fell on his ass.

Then they both disappeared into a hole. I had channeled earth, focusing on a circle around them, and dropped both men and the desk to the floor below. The rumble shook the building.

After kicking out the grate, I used the edge of the vent as a handhold and swung down to the floor near the hole.

Then we heard fire alarms and sprinklers went off. I hadn't done that, and the collapse hadn't started a fire, so I assumed that was Olivia or Woody's work. I'd deal with that in a minute.

Cochoran was out cold, having smacked his jaw on the desk on the landing, and he was gonna need a very good fucking dentist to sort out the mess in his mouth. Maybe Shauna could recommend one. But Toberman was getting up, covered in drywall and insulation.

He channeled at me, and I met it, because he tried to rupture the floor beneath me and thus have me collapse into the hole. I countered and stabilized the floor, at the same time channeling wind into the hole.

"No!" he shouted as suddenly objects began flying at tornado like speed. He tried to fling a few out at me with some success, but I dodged 'em.

He was at a *huge* disadvantage. I was in the open, relatively speaking, while he was confined in the small room below and in the hole. Basically, he was a bug in the bottom of the drain, and I was blowing wind down on him.

And water, because the fucking sprinklers kept going.

Finally, a brass bookend shaped like a dolphin slammed him right in the temple and he dropped like a rock. I cut the channeling fast, then jumped into the hole. I landed on the desk, which was stable but wet, still covered in papers and now drywall chunks.

I checked on them both. They were well out. I drugged them anyhow.

And as I finished that, Olivia arrived. Breathlessly, she said, "The girl is okay. She's tied up next door."

"Have you heard from your puppet?" I asked.

"Marionette," said Woody as he raced in. "I took him out easy. I almost pissed myself laughing."

"At what?"

"His face when I dove at him with a knife. Hold on."

He went to a computer and cut the sprinklers. "I set 'em off when I set fire to one of the storage rooms as a distraction."

"You needed a distraction for the driver?" I asked.

"No, I set it in case you needed one. I figured I was racing up here to bail both your pretty asses out. But you did good, kid. I might make a real superheroine out of the Cube yet."

I gave him the one-finger salute.

"What a mess," said Olivia.

"Never mind that," I said, looking at the papers on the desk. "If they were meeting here like this, these papers must be important. I took pictures, but I don't know how good they'll be."

"Yeah, they probably have clues," said Olivia.

"Definitely. Lemme take a look," said Woody.

Woody stood on the desk in the hole. Some of the papers had gone flying and gotten soaked or destroyed in the battle, but most of them were there as they were held in a file and pinned to the desk with a clip. Woody didn't say anything, quickly looking through them as we waited for about thirty very anxious seconds before he said, "At a glance, it looks like they were doing more than moving teenage girls. They were engaged in some financial chicanery here that was probably funding the cult, but I ain't an expert, and I'm sure this isn't all of it."

"What now?" asked Olivia. We were crouching on the edge of the hole. "We call the cops?"

"No way. They can't handle Toberman. Ops has to put him in a hole and then figure it out."

Olivia nodded. "I agree."

"So do I, for what it's worth."

I called Medina. She answered sounding kind of sleepy, which makes sense. It was pretty late for normal working calls. "Shelby?"

"Uh, hi. I need some help cleaning up a mess."

She paused, then said, "Where are you?"

"Local." I gave her the address and said, "We have a paranormal here, Toberman. Olivia kicked his ass. I kicked some butt, too, but Toberman is our main problem."

"Do the cops know?"

"Not yet. They were selling a teenage girl and doing some financial deals with six even seven figures moving around. We snuck in. They don't have any internal alarms on because, well, it's hard to engage in white slavery with cameras on."

She chuckled. "True. I have someone who is nearby. Sit tight for ten, fifteen minutes?"

"We got time and bottled water. We'll wait."

"Is the girl okay?"

"Yeah, a little shocked, but they didn't hurt her, just dragged her ass here."

"Who is she?"

"Don't know. She's still tied up. I mean, we had to ambush them and just finished. We'll take care of her now."

"Okay. I'll text you an ETA for our agent."

"Right. Thanks."

"No problem."

Once she hung up, I looked at Olivia. Woody was studying the papers, despite his claim, curious about the financial moves.

"BFFs, someone on the way, maybe fifteen. Let's check on the girl."

"Yes, I'm sure she's scared shitless," said Olivia. She was trying to untangle a knot in her hair.

Leaving Woody to his studies, we went to the room where the girl was held, tied to a chair and gagged. Her eyes widened when she saw me. After all, I looked like a superheroine and Olivia looked like, well, you know, just anyone else.

I removed the gag while Olivia worked on the ropes. The girl said, "You're the Cube!"

"Yeah," I said, a little embarrassed. "Who are you?"

"Mindy McGovern."

"Nice to meet you, Mindy. We're here to rescue you."

"Great," she said.

Once she was untied, she rose and grabbed Olivia's arm to steady herself, because she was stiff.

Or at least, that's what we thought she was doing.

Next thing we know, Olivia is flying back into the corridor and a chair flew across the room and slammed into my head. I go flying backwards and Olivia skids out the door. The door slams shut, locks, and I'm locked in this break room with a kid staring at me with a look of hatred you can't imagine.

She says nothing, just starts using TK to hurl chairs and furniture at me, while behind her one of the kitchen cabinet drawers opens and knives rise up.

I use elemental channeling and blow away the furniture and send an earth channel across the floor at Mindy.

It stops halfway.

This is what's known in the superheroine handbook as fucking trouble.

The knives start flying at me next. I suddenly have newfound pity for those magician assistants who stand there while knives are being flung at them. Oh, sure, Olivia has told me that's all a trick and how it's done, not that I'm telling you, but shit, this is the real thing. And Mindy the psycho kid can fling them with TK like a baseball pitcher flinging a fastball, easily hitting 100 M.P.H.

Wait, you say, the Cube is wearing Kevlar. Who cares about a bunch of knives? Well, Kevlar doesn't turn me into Supergirl. Quick primer, because I'm busy: Kevlar is a mix of materials that warp around anything that penetrates it to repel the force, which prevents penetration. I still feel the impact. It's why I don't wade into a hail of gunfire like fucking Batman.

Knives can be worse than bullets, actually. They're pointed. Bullets should have more force, but not in direct combat, and not when flung at 100 M.P.H. by a TM. Kevlar isn't completely stab resistant. Not that I'm some psycho combat expert. I'm just telling you what the salesperson in LA told me when I bought the shit.

What this means is, well, I'm a sitting duck.

"Aghhhhhhhhhhhhhhhh!" I scream as the knives fly at me and I dive behind a table that was knocked over when the chairs went flying.

Olivia is banging at the door. "God damn it, open this up!"

I have one edge: these aren't tactical knives. They're kitchen knives, and frankly most of them are past their prime. Even at this speed, as long as I don't just stand there and let psycho girl drive them home, I'm safe. The table blocks a lot of them, I knock down a couple with my arm, and a couple hit me but don't do more than sting.

I hear Olivia slamming the door with something.

Psycho Mindy keeps up the pressure, but she was counting on surprise, and I stopped her surprise attack. I've got the edge now. I quickly channel wind not at her, but at the table behind her and fling it like a frisbee into her back.

"Awkkkkkkk!" she yelps.

That sends her flying at me.

She tries to channel, but I have her in a wind corridor and she's disorganized.

Batter up!

As she comes at me, I strike out and punch her hard in the right side. Two ribs crack. She flies to my right like a rag doll, wailing.

Then she surprises me. She grabs my wind via TK and directs it at the window, shattering it, and uses that to glide down.

I scramble after her. I channel earth at the ground below, but she dodges and runs for the parking lot. She has to be really good to channel wind to enable her to glide down like that.

I race outside to the door, but it's not just locked, it's jammed, the walls probably shifting from my attempted earth channel. "Fuck! Olivia, it's blocked! Crazy girl is in the parking lot! Go!

"On it!"

Olivia races downstairs, while I step back and focus an earth channel on the ground to jar the door open. It takes two tries, but it works. I also realize I have two knives stuck in me, one in my right thigh, on in my upper right arm. Adrenaline is a great thing.

Racing to the parking lot, I find Olivia standing at the edge of it, looking around like someone had pinched her butt.

"Well?" I asked, out of breath. I need more cardio in my workouts.

"She's long gone. I can't even sense her aura. She's fast as a deer, or she has some type of screening," said Olivia, pouting.

"Maybe both."

"Do we go after her?" Olivia asked.

"No, we gotta check on Woody and find out what was going on here. I mean, the two of us wandering Vegas trying to find a teenage girl is a needle in a haystack type of proposition."

"Yeah."

We raced back upstairs, but cautiously. When we arrived at the penthouse, we found Woody studying two orange rocks he'd found somewhere and placed on the windowsill. They were about the size of pencil eraser.

"What are those?" I asked.

"Gems. Dunno what they do, though."

"I feel power radiating from them," said Olivia. As if mesmerized, she reached out to touch them.

Woody stopped her. "I wouldn't. Is Ops still on the way?"

I nodded. "Someone named McTaggert will be here in five minutes, tops."

"They need to deal with this thing. As for the papers, I've taken pics. We can work on that. Where's the girl?"

Olivia and I looked at each other. Then we each pointed at the other and said, "She fucked up."

Epilogue

The net result of this shitstorm was the teenage girl who obviously wasn't a teenage girl, or was in on it, or whatever the fuck happened, got away clean. I let Medina know. Woody and I would work on trying to find her, but we weren't optimistic.

Toberman and Cochran were taken into custody by Ops, because Toberman was paranormal. Ops is a military organization, so they can hold people pretty much for anything. It's convenient, but a little scary. However, they learn nothing we didn't already know. Toberman was moving money for the cult. But he wasn't the top like we thought. We were closer, but not there. Toberman and Cochran knew Flannagan on an abstract level, but neither of them had a contact method, or so they claimed. They didn't even know where he lived. Barry knew next to nothing. Davis died in the hospital. The Rowes knew nothing of Flannagan.

Our only lead to the mysterious Flannagan now appeared to be the teenage girl. Which sucked, because we didn't know her real name. The name she gave me was clearly a fake. And we didn't know anything about her or how to find her.

Woody was really down.

Three days later, Olivia and I cheered him up. I went to this local comic shop and found a plastic replica ring that belongs to some superhero named Green Lantern. When I came home, he was sitting on the couch watching a movie.

"I miss popcorn," he muttered.

Following the lead of my text, she came out of the bedroom and said, "We have something better."

We approached him on the couch, then I handed him the ring. "Welcome to the team, Woody."

He looked at the ring, then laughed. "Aw, man, you broads are something else. Here I thought you were gonna make me get a real job!"

Olivia laughed. "Yeah, well, you are fired from my act! I need you here stopping crime!"

I laughed. "He was the worst part of your act anyhow."

Olivia nodded and he gave her the finger.

Then I said, "We'll help your people, find your sister, okay? I've done weirder shit."

"Yeah, like what?"

I thought for a minute, then said, "I once had a guy stick a carrot up my butt and then he ate it."

"Ewwwwwwwwwwwwwwwwwwwwwww!" said Olivia.

Woody laughed.

Oh, yeah, and then Olivia and I spent a night together before she went on a big, ten-day show swing in Utah. I would miss her. We really made serious, close love, grateful we were okay. It wasn't sex. It was well beyond that.

As we sat in bed after, I said, "I should write this shit down."

"You could never publish it, but I bet it would be good reading," said Olivia with a laugh.

"You never know. When I'm eighty and need more plastic surgery to look forty, I could sell it and be rich."

She laughed. "You're a nut." Then she rolled over and kissed me. "My nut."

"I'm yours when I'm not a nut. The Cube is the nut. But she's the one that keeps everyone safe out there so they can read this shit."

Olivia kissed me. "I'm sorry I have this trip now."

"Hey, baby, this is your career. This is important. Besides, Woody and I will be fine. It will be like a sitcom, y'know, hooker teamed with voodoo doll. NBC would buy it in a second."

"I doubt that."

"We'll be fine. Trust me. Nothing is going to happen."

Which, of course, is fucking *not* how that ever turns out.

But that is a story for another day, because it's late and I'm going to fucking bed. You should too, unless you're too buy jacking off.

Out.